Enlightened Horizons

Enlightened Horizons
Shining a light on Indigenous North Americans

ISBN 9781609621841(Enlightened Horizons: Shining a light on Indigenous North Americans, Happy Cloud Press, 150, paperback cover, perfect binding, 5.5 x 8.5 dimensions)

ISBN 9781609621841

9 781609 621841

90000 >

Members of Editorial Team: Jonelle Alvarado Perez (Managing Editor), Tessa Faust (Design Director), Stone McGuire (Marketing Director), Sarah Kee (Acquisitions Editor), and Cecelia Bialas (Copy Editor)

Cover photo by Tessa Faust

Printed by UNL Printing

For the Indigenous writers, whose work appears in this anthology, and their families.

Special thanks to Dr. Beverley Rilett, UNL Printing, Dr. Paul Royster, and Mr. T.J. Jochum for their assistance in the creation of this anthology.

Contents

Editors' Introduction

The texts included within this anthology revolve around the theme of Indigenous identity before and after European settlement and colonization in North America. The intended purpose of this book is to help with the celebration, preservation, and reclamation of Indigenous culture by selecting pieces written about or by Indigenous writers before 1925. The following Indigenous tribes are represented in this anthology, in no particular order: Dog-ribs, Winnebago, Algonquin, Mohawk, Sioux, Santee Sioux, Dakota, Santee Dakota, Yankton Dakota, Hopi, Meskwaki, Nakoaktok, Omaha, and Ojibwe.

The anthology is mapped out in an attempt to show the gradual progression of the effect of colonization on Indigenous identities. In order to accomplish this, the anthology is structured so that the reader can see the effects of European settlement and colonization as they progress from one text to the next. However, it is important to note that the progression is not meant to be a perfect chronological history of the effects of colonialism or North American Indigenous history, but rather a representation of how Indigenous lifestyles were affected, along with the subsequent process of reclaiming their heritage. All of the tribes included in this anthology were affected by westward expansion; using the collective stories and experiences of Indigenous communities native to North America demonstrates how their identities have changed and been influenced by the presence of European colonialism.

The anthology begins with several images of different Indigenous communities in ceremonial attire, before transitioning to nonfiction and Indigenous stories. The middle portion features different poems and legends from Indigenous writers, before transitioning to works that focus more heavily on conforming to a Western lifestyle, as evidenced by Zitkala-Ša's essays within The School Days of an Indian Girl that depict her experiences at a boarding school, along with her assimilation into western culture. Two newspaper articles, "Lo the poor indian prospers" and "Uncle Sam's Indian Wards," have also been included for similar purposes of illustrating the pressure that Indigenous communities felt to assimilate into American culture in the latter half of the anthology. However, these articles contain a more prejudiced view towards Indigenous groups, but the editors felt it was important to show the opinions that many Americans held during this time period and how these beliefs affected many Americans' interactions with Indigenous men and women. The final two selections in the anthology provide a sense of optimism for the reader by focusing on Native pride and the embracement of Indigenous culture with Zitkala-Sa's essay "Why I am Pagan" and Jane Johnston Schoolcraft's poem "Invocation." It is intended to offer hope for the preservation of Indigenous culture and voices for future generations to learn about and preserve their heritage.

While the included texts end with Jane Johnston Schoolcrafts' poem "Invocation," the editors of this anthology decided to include a final section at the end of the anthology to provide more information and resources to learn more about Indigenous communities in North America, and about some of the issues that they are facing in this present climate. These include a large number of missing and murdered Indigenous Women (MMIW) in their communities, and also being disproportionately affected by Covid-19 (e.g. Covid-19 Emergency Response Fund). More information is included on these topics in the back of the anthology, along with ways to volunteer or donate to organizations that are directly combating these issues.

Kotsuis and Hohhug-Nakoaktok, wearing ceremonial dress, with long beaks, on their haunches, dancing photographed by Edward S. Curtis

HOW MESKWAKI CHILDREN SHOULD BE BROUGHT UP

DICTATED BY HARRY LINCOLN OF THE MESKWAKI

WRITTEN BY TRUMAN MICHELSON

When a boy becomes old enough to be intelligent, his parents begin to teach him how to take care of himself and act righteously. They usually tell him not to do a good many things. Children are taught not to be naughty. They are told that if they are naughty, people will have nothing to do with them. They are told that if they are naughty, people will talk about them. And children are told not to steal anything from their neighbors. Moreover, children are taught not to talk to people. If they see any one going by their place, they should hold their tongues, nor should they laugh.

And they also tell children not to visit other people too often. "Every time they see you going anywhere they would say that you are looking for something good to eat, if you go visiting too often," is what children are told. So children do not often visit too much.

They likewise tell children not to gamble. They tell them that they might be lucky and win, but that it would not benefit them. And they tell them that it is just as bad to lose. They caution them in this way: "If you win, people will see your winnings and will try to get you to gamble. And if you do, you will surely lose all that you have won. And yet it is not right to be over-quiet. If you are quiet and well off, that is not quite right either. If you have a lot of horses, people will be jealous of you. Some one might want some of your property, and you would not give it to him. That is how it will be.

"The best way is to be kindly to everyone, to speak kind words, to treat your friends nicely, to keep your heart clean, and not to talk meanly. If you do this, you will have a number of friends. And when you are a young boy, do not fight with

3

other boys. If any one speaks badly to you, do not answer him. Let it go. This is one of the best things you can do. And if you see someone doing something, you must hold your peace; do not be the one to start the news. Do not tell what you saw him or her do. If you spread the report they will hate you. They will become your enemies."

And there is another thing which boys are told. Boys are told not to tattle to any one. They are told not to be too intimate with girls. It is not a right thing for a boy to do. They are warned: "If you do that, people will be jealous of you."

And there is another thing they are warned. "When there are many people, when something is going on, don't go over there, and try to show off. That will not benefit you. You may go to the crowd and see what is going on, but behave yourself. And if any one asks you a question, you are to tell the person that you know nothing about it. That is the best way to keep out of trouble."

And there is another thing which young men are told, which is: "If some one asks you to do a favor, you must always do it for him. Some time in the near future they will come around again and ask another favor of you. If you refuse, you straightway will begin to have trouble. But you should always do a favor for any one, so as to please them."

And another thing, young men are told, not to fear ashes: "By fasting and painting your face with ashes, you may get a blessing from the Manitou. If you do the right thing, you will surely be blessed. If you are afraid, the Manitou will know it. People claim that fasting and blackening one's face with ashes is one of the best things that they can do. In the early days it was said that if one fasted long to obtain a blessing from the Manitou, he often went on the war-path successfully; or he killed people by fasting so long. Such was the blessing the person obtained. And you can go and kill game easily. You may become a leader in anything. If there is a war you may become a leader. And you will always bring your men back safe and sound. They will not be killed by the enemy. You will surely be blessed by the Manitou if you take an interest in fasting, and are not afraid of doing so. After you have fasted long enough, if you desire anything, you will obtain it. So fasting is the right thing to do. And if you do this, you must get up early—before our grandfather, the Sun, rises. If anything happens to people where you are, after a few years, nothing will happen to you: you will not be destroyed. This is the only way you can live again. All the people will be benefited by you. This is the best life there is." And this is why children are taught to fast.

Boys are told that if they see an animal they must not destroy it. For if they destroy animals, they themselves will not live very long. Boys are also taught to be good hunters.

Boys are taught nearly everything so that they can get along nicely with their wives after they are married. They are told that if they are hustlers many girls will wish to marry them.

Of course this is after they have grown to be young men. Up to that time they are merely made to fast. And by fasting, is how they reach old age. Also children are made to fast when any one dies. And they also tell children not to make a noise when some one dies; and not to play where the body is. And they tell boys not to refuse if they are asked to do something. "If you do what people who have lost their relatives ask you, they will be well satisfied with you. And some day you will exchange positions. If you ask them a favor at that time, they will willingly do it," is what boys are told.

And this is what boys are told when they are growing up: "If you are asked to be a ceremonial attendant at clan festivals, you must do it. By doing them the favor of waiting on them, you will benefit your own life. And any time you are asked to do anything you must always do it, so as to please the people."

And after they grow up, they are told not to bother too much with girls, especially if they have sisters of their own. They are told, "Sometime you may be desired as a son-in-law.

But if you bother with many girls, while going with one, they will think you are a nobody." And they tell boys not to be intimate with girls unless they plan to marry them. They are told, "You must not say anything evil to women: if you do, you will be talking evilly to your own sisters.

"And if you are going with a girl, if you are engaged to her, you must marry her, and treat her rightly. You must go home with her and stay with your father-in-law and your mother-in-law. You must treat them as nicely as you can. And you should hunt for your mother-in-law and your father-in-law. If you treat your wife meanly, every one will talk about you. And that will make it bad for you. At all gatherings people will talk about you, saying how badly you treat your wife. The people will say many things about you, though you may not know it. They will say you are jealous. And in that way people will always refuse you favors. You will be treating your wife badly, if you pay no attention to the old people.

"You must obey your parents. It is the right thing to obey one's parents. And boys who do not obey their parents are the worst boys to-day.

"If you know any one has something of his own, you must not ask him for it, nor must you steal it. It is not right to steal. If you steal or ask for the thing you want, all the people will be afraid of you. You are nothing but a beggar. Every one will say that to you. They will call you a beggar."

Now when boys are beginning to be grown up, they are told: "You must not turn against your friends; you must be kind-hearted. And you must not bother with any woman or girl who is married to another man. You should not try to 'cut him out.' It is dangerous to do that." This is one of the most important things they try to get boys to understand. By doing what is forbidden they might get into trouble; and they might end their lives. Many boys end their lives before they are middle-aged by not listening to their parents.

And girls are taught a little differently from boys. Of

course they tell girls, in the beginning, the same thing, that is, how to take care of themselves. They teach girls that if they obey the rules they will have an easier life as they grow older. After they are old enough they teach them how to do things. And they also make them fast. They are asked to fast so that adversity shall not strike them when they grow up. They make girls fast for four days. They make them fast all winter, especially when they are beginning to be young ladies. The reason why they make them fast is that they are supposed to dream of something that will take them through their life. That is why they do not take regular meals like others, to prepare for a long life.

And they teach them to do something for themselves, especially when they grow up. They teach them work, suitable for women. They teach them to learn to make mattings and how to make sacks. They also teach them how to make moccasins and beadwork. Girls are told that they can get along nicely if they learn these things before they are married. They are told, "You will be benefited by doing this for your husband. Your relatives will be benefited by you."

And girls are told: "If you are a moral girl, your father-in-law and mother-in-law will treat you as nicely as they can. And they will love you. If you are quiet and well-behaved, you will be much better off than those girls who do not mind. Men do not care for girls who do not mind and who are immoral. If you do not mind and are immoral, no man will have you for his wife." That is why girls are taught to be good.

After they learn to make things, they are taught to cook meals. Girls are told that by doing so, they are leading themselves the right way. "By so doing you are leading yourself an easy way. Sometime you may grow up and make your own home." That is why girls are told to be willing workers.

And girls are told not to go off and live with other people. Of course people would like a girl to live with them a few days. But a few days later they might turn her out, especially if she were lazy. People do not wish to support a lazy person. This is why girls are taught to cook.

And after they are married, girls are especially told not to say anything about other persons, and not to feel unfriendly towards them. And they are told not to have any quarrels with other people, for that is not a right thing to do. They are told to be kind towards the people and not to have quarrels with any one. "This is the best way, to be friendly with every one. By so doing, the people will feel kindly towards you. They will always say a good word for you. People do not think anything of a mean person. If you are mean, some day some one will turn against you. Some persons are dangerous. They have secret ways to kill people." This is why girls are told not to be mean, or say mean things to other persons. And some girls hate their parents for telling them this. But it is a rule that children should be taught. The reason parents tell girls this, is because they love them so well. They are teaching them so they can attain an old age. Girls who were not taught, do anything they please. They do not care what they do. They spoil themselves.

Girls are supposed to be taught till they are married. After a girl is married, she has full control of herself, and may do whatever she thinks best. But it is best to follow the rules forever, to be kind to one's husband and the people. It is pretty hard to lead a righteous life.

When girls begin to have children they are told to be kind to their children and love them, and not to do anything bad to them. And they are taught that if they live quietly to an old age, they themselves will be the only relations they have.

And before children are well grown, they dare not go any place by themselves. Of course boys are different: they can go any place they please. And girls dare not do so, unless they have a good reason for it. They are taught to always be at home and do the work. They are told: "If you grow to be a young lady, if you walk around and do not do any work, people will not think anything of you. They will always talk about you. They will say that all you are good for, is to walk from place to place.

They will say you are looking for a place to get your meals. They will say that you are looking for a place where you can get the finest food. They will say many things about you. They will even say that you are worse than a man. Every time you are on the road they will say, 'There goes a woman who goes about looking for good meals for herself.'" That is the reason why they desire a girl to be able to do things so that she can support herself after she is grown. That is why they tell girls to obey their parents. Their parents have had good experience and know what they are talking about.

And when girls arrive at puberty, they are told not to marry a divorced man. They are told to marry a young man. In the early days, people used to say to each other when girls married divorced men: "It is not natural for a girl to marry a divorced man, nor for a young man to marry a divorced woman." They told girls that if they married young men, that they would be benefited by getting horses, and so on. And a girl is told to look around and get the right kind of a boy. In the early days, they liked boys who killed game, trapped, sold furs, and so got money; but nowadays they tell girls to look around for boys that have horses, homes, everything they want. They say, "That's the right kind of a young man to marry—one that can support you."

Girls are also told: "When you are staying with your father-in-law and with your mother-in-law, you are supposed to help them in their work. When your mother-in-law begins doing anything, you must ask her if you may do it." A girl is taught this so that she can get along nicely after she is married. Girls are told: "If you don't do these things, people will talk about you, and say how lazy you are. And people will not like you." This is the reason why a girl is taught all manner of work.

And all girls are taught the same things. And in this way, they lead themselves the right way.

The Masked Kachinas (Hopi Indian "Rainmakers"), Village of Shonghopavi, Arizona
photographed by Underwood & Underwood

THE BADGER AND THE BEAR

RETOLD BY ZITKALA-SA

On the edge of a forest there lived a large family of badgers. In the ground their dwelling was made. Its walls and roof were covered with rocks and straw.

Old father badger was a great hunter. He knew well how to track the deer and buffalo. Every day he came home carrying on his back some wild game. This kept mother badger very busy, and the baby badgers very chubby. While the well-fed children played about, digging little make-believe dwellings, their mother hung thin sliced meats upon long willow racks. As fast as the meats were dried and seasoned by sun and wind, she packed them carefully away in a large thick bag.

This bag was like a huge stiff envelope, but far more beautiful to see, for it was painted all over with many bright colors. These firmly tied bags of dried meat were laid upon the rocks in the walls of the dwelling. In this way they were both useful and decorative.

One day father badger did not go off for a hunt. He stayed at home, making new arrows. His children sat about him on the ground floor. Their small black eyes danced with delight as they watched the gay colors painted upon the arrows.

All of a sudden there was heard a heavy footfall near the entrance way. The oval-shaped door-frame was pushed aside. In stepped a large black foot with great big claws. Then the other clumsy foot came next. All the while the baby badgers stared hard at the unexpected comer. After the second foot, in peeped the head of a big black bear! His black nose was dry and parched. Silently he entered the dwelling and sat down on the ground by the doorway. His black eyes never left the painted bags on the rocky walls. He guessed what was in them. He was a very hungry bear. Seeing the racks of red meat hanging in the yard, he had come to visit the badger family.

Though he was a stranger and his strong paws and jaws

11

frightened the small badgers, the father said, "How, how, friend! Your lips and nose look feverish and hungry. Will you eat with us?"

"Yes, my friend," said the bear. "I am starved. I saw your racks of red fresh meat, and knowing your heart is kind, I came hither. Give me meat to eat, my friend."

Hereupon the mother badger took long strides across the room, and as she had to pass in front of the strange visitor, she said: "Ah han! Allow me to pass!" which was an apology.

"How, how!" replied the bear, drawing himself closer to the wall and crossing his shins together.

Mother badger chose the most tender red meat, and soon over a bed of coals she broiled the venison.

That day the bear had all he could eat. At nightfall he rose, and smacking his lips together—that is the noisy way of saying "the food was very good!"—he left the badger dwelling. The baby badgers, peeping through the door-flap after the shaggy bear, saw him disappear into the woods near by.   Day after day the crackling of twigs in the forest told of heavy footsteps. Out would come the same black bear. He never lifted the door-flap, but thrusting it aside entered slowly in. Always in the same place by the entrance way he sat down with crossed shins.

His daily visits were so regular that mother badger placed a fur rug in his place. She did not wish a guest in her dwelling to sit upon the bare hard ground.

At last one time when the bear returned, his nose was bright and black. His coat was glossy. He had grown fat upon the badger's hospitality.

As he entered the dwelling a pair of wicked gleams shot out of his shaggy head. Surprised by the strange behavior of the guest who remained standing upon the rug, leaning his round back against the wall, father badger queried: "How, my friend! What?"

The bear took one stride forward and shook his paw in the badger's face. He said: "I am strong, very strong!"

"Yes, yes, so you are," replied the badger. From the farther end of the room mother badger muttered over her bead work: "Yes, you grew strong from our well-filled bowls."

The bear smiled, showing a row of large sharp teeth.

"I have no dwelling. I have no bags of dried meat. I have no arrows. All these I have found here on this spot," said he, stamping his heavy foot. "I want them! See! I am strong!" repeated he, lifting both his terrible paws.

Quietly the father badger spoke: "I fed you. I called you friend, though you came here a stranger and a beggar. For the sake of my little ones leave us in peace."

Mother badger, in her excited way, had pierced hard through the buckskin and stuck her fingers repeatedly with her sharp awl until she had laid aside her work. Now, while her husband was talking to the bear, she motioned with her hands to the children. On tiptoe they hastened to her side.

For reply came a low growl. It grew louder and more fierce. "Wa-ough!" he roared, and by force hurled the badgers out. First the father badger; then the mother. The little badgers he tossed by pairs. He threw them hard upon the ground. Standing in the entrance way and showing his ugly teeth, he snarled, "Be gone!"

The father and mother badger, having gained their feet, picked up their kicking little babes, and, wailing aloud, drew the air into their flattened lungs till they could stand alone upon their feet. No sooner had the baby badgers caught their breath than they howled and shrieked with pain and fright. Ah! what a dismal cry was theirs as the whole badger family went forth wailing from out their own dwelling! A little distance away from their stolen house the father badger built a small round hut. He made it of bent willows and covered it with dry grass and twigs.

This was shelter for the night; but alas! it was empty of food and arrows. All day father badger prowled through the forest, but without his arrows he could not get food for his children. Upon his return, the cry of the little ones for meat, the sad quiet of the mother with bowed head, hurt him like a poisoned arrow wound.

"I'll beg meat for you!" said he in an unsteady voice. Covering his head and entire body in a long loose robe he halted beside the big black bear. The bear was slicing red meat to hang upon the rack. He did not pause for a look at the comer. As the badger stood there unrecognized, he saw that the bear had brought with him his whole family. Little cubs played under the high-hanging new meats. They laughed and pointed with their wee noses upward at the thin sliced meats upon the poles.

"Have you no heart, Black Bear? My children are starving. Give me a small piece of meat for them," begged the badger.

"Wa-ough!" growled the angry bear, and pounced upon the badger. "Be gone!" said he, and with his big hind foot he sent father badger sprawling on the ground.

All the little ruffian bears hooted and shouted "ha-ha!" to see the beggar fall upon his face. There was one, however, who did not even smile. He was the youngest cub. His fur coat was not as black and glossy as those his elders wore. The hair was dry and dingy. It looked much more like kinky wool. He was the ugly cub. Poor little baby bear! he had always been laughed at by his older brothers. He could not help being himself. He could not change the differences between himself and his brothers. Thus again, though the rest laughed aloud at the badger's fall, he did not see the joke. His face was long and earnest. In his heart he was sad to see the badgers crying and starving. In his breast spread a burning desire to share his food with them.

"I shall not ask my father for meat to give away. He would say 'No!' Then my brothers would laugh at me," said the ugly baby bear to himself.

In an instant, as if his good intention had passed from him, he was singing happily and skipping around his father at work. Singing in his small high voice and dragging his feet in long strides after him, as if a prankish spirit oozed out from his heels, he strayed off through the tall grass. He was ambling toward the small round hut. When directly in front of the entrance way, he made a quick side kick with his left hind leg. Lo! there fell into the badger's hut a piece of fresh meat. It was tough meat, full of sinews, yet it was the only piece he could take without his father's notice.

Thus having given meat to the hungry badgers, the ugly baby bear ran quickly away to his father again.

On the following day the father badger came back once more. He stood watching the big bear cutting thin slices of meat.

"Give—" he began, when the bear turning upon him with a growl, thrust him cruelly aside. The badger fell on his hands. He fell where the grass was wet with the blood of the newly carved buffalo. His keen starving eyes caught sight of a little red clot lying bright upon the green. Looking fearfully toward the bear and seeing his head was turned away, he snatched up the small thick blood. Underneath his girdled blanket he hid it in his hand.

On his return to his family, he said within himself: "I'll pray the Great Spirit to bless it." Thus he built a small round lodge. Sprinkling water upon the heated heap of sacred stones within, he made ready to purge his body. "The buffalo blood, too, must be purified before I ask a blessing upon it," thought the badger. He carried it into the sacred vapor lodge. After placing it near the sacred stones, he sat down beside it. After a long silence, he muttered: "Great Spirit, bless this little buffalo blood." Then he arose, and with a quiet dignity stepped out of the lodge. Close behind him some one followed. The badger turned to look over his shoulder and to his great joy he beheld a Dakota brave in handsome buckskins. In his hand he carried a magic arrow. Across his back dangled a long fringed quiver. In answer to the badger's prayer, the avenger had sprung from out the red globules.

"My son!" exclaimed the badger with extended right hand.

"How, father," replied the brave; "I am your avenger!"

Immediately the badger told the sad story of his hungry little ones and the stingy bear.

Listening closely the young man stood looking steadily upon the ground.

At length the father badger moved away. [return]

"Where?" queried the avenger. [return]

"My son, we have no food. I am going again to beg for meat," answered the badger. [return]

"Then I go with you," replied the young brave. This made the old badger happy. He was proud of his son. He was delighted to be called "father" by the first human creature.

The bear saw the badger coming in the distance. He narrowed his eyes at the tall stranger walking beside him. He spied the arrow. At once he guessed it was the avenger of whom he had heard long, long ago. As they approached, the bear stood erect with a hand on his thigh. He smiled upon them. [return]

"How, badger, my friend! Here is my knife. Cut your favorite pieces from the deer," said he, holding out a long thin blade.

"How!" said the badger eagerly. He wondered what had inspired the big bear to such a generous deed. The young avenger waited till the badger took the long knife in his hand.

Gazing full into the black bear's face, he said: "I come to do justice. You have returned only a knife to my poor father. Now return to him his dwelling." His voice was deep and powerful. In his black eyes burned a steady fire.

The long strong teeth of the bear rattled against each other, and his shaggy body shook with fear. "Ahow!" cried he, as if he had been shot. Running into the dwelling he gasped, breathless and trembling, "Come out, all of you! This is the badger's dwelling. We must flee to the forest for fear of the avenger who carries the magic arrow."

Out they hurried, all the bears, and disappeared into the woods.

Singing and laughing, the badgers returned to their own dwelling.

Then the avenger left them.

"I go," said he in parting, "over the earth."

AS RED MEN DIE

BY E. PAULINE JOHNSON

Captive! Is there a hell to him like this?
A taunt more galling than the Huron's hiss?
He—proud and scornful, he—who laughed at law,
He—scion of the deadly Iroquois,
He—the bloodthirsty, he—the Mohawk chief,
He—who despises pain and sneers at grief,
Here in the hated Huron's vicious clutch,
That even captive he disdains to touch!

Captive! But *never* conquered; Mohawk brave
Stoops not to be to *any* man a slave;
Least, to the puny tribe his soul abhors,
The tribe whose wigwams sprinkle Simcoe's shores.
With scowling brow he stands and courage high,
Watching with haughty and defiant eye
His captors, as they council o'er his fate,
Or strive his boldness to intimidate.
Then fling they unto him the choice;

"Wilt thou
Walk o'er the bed of fire that waits thee now—
Walk with uncovered feet upon the coals
Until thou reach the ghostly Land of Souls,
And, with thy Mohawk death-song please our ear?
Or wilt thou with the women rest thee here?"
His eyes flash like an eagle's, and his hands
Clench at the insult. Like a god he stands.
"Prepare the fire!" he scornfully demands.
He knoweth not that this same jeering band
Will bite the dust—will lick the Mohawk's hand;
Will kneel and cower at the Mohawk's feet;
Will shrink when Mohawk war-drums wildly beat.

His death will be avenged with hideous hate
By Iroquois, swift to annihilate
His vile detested captors, that now flaunt
Their war clubs in his face with sneer and taunt,
Not thinking, soon that reeking, red, and raw,
Their scalps will deck the belts of Iroquois.

The path of coals outstretches, white with heat,
A forest fir's length—ready for his feet.
Unflinching as a rock he steps along
The burning mass, and sings his wild war song;
Sings, as he sang when once he used to roam
Throughout the forests of his southern home,
Where, down the Genesee, the water roars,
Where gentle Mohawk purls between its shores,
Songs, that of exploit and of prowess tell;
Songs of the Iroquois invincible.

Up the long trail of fire he boasting goes,
Dancing a war dance to defy his foes.
His flesh is scorched, his muscles burn and shrink,
But still he dances to death's awful brink.
The eagle plume that crests his haughty head
Will never droop until his heart be dead.
Slower and slower yet his footstep swings,
Wilder and wilder still his death-song rings,
Fiercer and fiercer thro' the forest bounds
His voice that leaps to Happier Hunting Grounds.
One savage yell—

Then loyal to his race,
He bends to death—but *never* to disgrace.

Hopi Katcinas drawn by Kutcahanauu (White-Bear)

METEMPSYCHOSIS.

BY ELI L HUGGINS

I.

I was a huntsman in my youth, and knew
Each bird and beast that haunts the forest tall,
Or wings the air, hard by the water-fall.
Over the plain and up the mountain blue
My twanging bow was heard, my arrows flew.
My bowstring now is rent, my arrows all
Like spears that from the withered pine-cones fall,
Have from my shrunken quiver vanished too.
Yet sometimes o'er me steals the olden mood,
And wandering in the forest deep and dark,
I greet each old familiar tree and mark,
Each spot whereon the lovely quarry stood,
While faintly through my withered veins once more
Leaps the triumphant thrill I knew of yore.

II.

I shot an arrow through the wood one day
In idle sport, and following where it led,
I found a doe that I had raised and fed,
Stricken, and bleeding fast her life away,
Her tender fawn transfixed beside her lay;
One random shaft two happy lives had sped.
The dry leaves rustled to my startled tread,
And filled my fluttering heart with strange dismay;
For gazing in those failing eyes my soul
Found there another soul, its very twin;
Unseen for years, but bowered deep within
The heart's alcove,—oh, lost beyond control!
Those murdered eyes still gaze as from a glass
Framed in with bloody leaves and trampled grass.

WHY THE PINE TREES WEEP

AN OJIBWAY LEGEND

BY WILLIAM EDGAR BROWN

A beautiful story to me was told
Of the days when the earth was new;
It told how the Indian race begun,
In that wonderful land of the Rising Sun,
And the clime where the pine trees grew;
It told me of Mongo, the Manitou Man;
And the days when the earth was new.

It told me that Mongo, the Manitou Man,
Left his home to return no more;
And wandered far north where the wild winds blow,
And the forest glistens with ice and snow,
On the bleak Superior shore;
Where the howl of the gray wolf lulled him to
sleep,
And the Escanabas roar.

No want was known in that wonderful land,
Where fish and game abound,
And the roaring camp-fire's cheerful glow,
Sent shadows flickering to and fro,
The forest dim around;
But the heart of Mongo was heavy and sad;
Who no companion found.

Great Spirit saw that his heart was sad,
So one night as he sat by the fire,
He saw in the heavens a meteor bright,
Which flashed through the sky like waves of light,
And it brought him his heart's desire;
For the bright ball fell and burst at his feet;
And it gave him his heart's desire.

For there a short distance from where he sat,
Stood a woman wondrous fair,
Who came from the heart of the ball of light,
With form so winsome and eyes so bright,
And a wealth of coal black hair.
And the meteor's sparks were not more bright,
Than the eyes of this maiden fair.

At first the heart of the Manitou Man,
Was startled, and filled with fear,
He stood in silence, his lips were dumb,
When she x held out her hands and beckoned to come,
And he tremblingly drew near.
Then his terror was changed to a passion of love,
As he felt her presence near.

The maiden was Masaqua (New Born Light),
Who had come to gladden his home;
So he led her away to his big tepee,
That she the light of his life might be,
And ne'er from him should roam;
But brighten his lodge by the light of her eyes,
Like the light when the bright star shone.

They dwelt together for many a moon,
And sons and daughters were born;
The echoing forest rang with their glee,
And their laughter gladdened the big tepee,
They shouted at early morn;
For their hearts were as light as the zephyrs that
blow
The leaves of the ripening corn.

One day, Mongo, the Manitou Man
Fell sick, and they feared he would die;
Though Wasaqua nursed him with tender care,
His spirit went home e'er she was aware
To the land of the cloudless sky.

And they made him a grave in a mossy dell;
In a glade where a brook flows by.
For Wasaqua, the New Born Light,
No comfort could be found;
She threw herself down on her loved one's grave,
And woeful lamentations made,
For with tears she suffused the ground;
No wild bird warbled his welcome notes
From the sombre woods around.

The bears and the wolves lay down by her side
To keep her warm at night;
The birds and beasts brought morsels rare
To nourish and show their tender care;
And the sun shed his wondrous light;
While the silvery moon-beams softly crept,
O'er the grave, in the lonesome night.

But she grieved, for her love had been tender and
strong,
'Twas a love that could never fail;
And she fell asleep as the sun went down,
And the fragrant breath of the flowers was blown
By the balmy southern gale;
And they made her a grave by her husband's side,
In the depth of the lonely vale.

The Whip-poor-will's voice was heard no more,
And the wolf's drear howl was still;
The great owl ceased his nightly song,
And the tall forest trees sighed all night long,
In grief for the ones who had gone;
And that lonely valley was draped with mist,
In the gray of the early dawn.

E'er the sun shone on the grave again,
A solitary pine,
A watchman seemed that towering stood,

The stately monarch of the wood,
Rising to height sublime,
Where the first man and woman were laid,
The first tree of its kind.

So night and day the pine tree wept;
And sang a sad refrain;
As lonely its faithful vigil it kept,
Above the graves where the loved ones slept,
Who would never come back again.
So unto this day do the pine trees weep,
And sing a sad refrain.

LEGEND OF THE NORTH STAR

AN OJIBWAY LEGEND

BY WILLIAM EDGAR BROWN

There lived in a lodge in the forest wide,
On the shore of the great wide sea,
Where the antlered dweller of the wild,
Roamed through the wild woods free,
Two brothers, who were friends indeed,
As brothers ought to be.

For many and many a moon they roamed,
To hunt the prowling bear;
And still their love the warmer grew,
Still loved they more to share
Each other's sorrows, joys, and grief;
And bear each other's care.

A pledge they made by the side of the sea,
That they would never part;
For the love that they loved would be steadfast
 love,
The love of a guileless heart,
A love that was born of friendship true,
And not deceptive art.

So hand in hand they journeyed on,
'Neath the heaven's wondrous blue,
Through the forest wide they wandered oft,
God's wondrous works to view,
And their hearts were happy as singing birds;
In the joy of their friendship true.

But soon a change came into their lives,
As has happened oft before;
For brothers like others their friendship fails,
As friendship has failed before;

For one of the brothers fell in love,
With a maid from a southern shore.

The lodge was too large for the grandmother old,
And the game too hard to dress;
So she asked two maidens to come and dwell,
In her lodge in the wilderness;
So one of the maidens won the heart,
Of the man that she loved best.

How listless now were the lives of the men,
Who had both been friends so true;
For one could shoot the prowling bear,
But naught could the other do,
But think of the maid who had come to his lodge,
The live long day all through.

For what can a man or maiden do,
When they deeply fall in love?
They are good for naught in this world below,
Nor fit for the world above;
Till they haste away, on their wedding day,
In the ardor of youthful love.

So seeing how badly his brother failed,
In killing the prowling bear,
He asked what change had come over his life
Or what was his weight of care.
'Twas then he confessed he had fallen in love,
With the maiden with coal black hair.

"If that be true," the brother replied,
I shall leave thee, brother dear,
I shall not return to my lodge again,
Nor to this forest drear;
So fare-thee-well ! my friend! farewell!
The Manitou's call I hear."

So saying, he started for the North,
Not waiting for reply;
No pleading words could halt his steps,
Or turn his steadfast eye;
But these were the words that floated back,
As he mounted up on high.

"Although I have gone to return no more,
Yet I'll ever be your friend,
And shine on high in the northern sky,
Till days and nights shall end,
And twinkle bright, in the North at night,
Then you'll know I am your friend.

If ever you're in the forest lost,
I hope you'll watch for me;
For I'll be thinking of you dear friend!
Where ever you may be;
And I will guide you safe home again;
To your lodge by the northern sea."

Thus saying, he began to mount,
Up! Up! to tbe northern sky;
Unto this day he is standing there,
Chasing the bear, hard by,
As he loved to do in the Michigan woods;
So he still does in the sky.

The other hunter was so chagrined
That he turned in sore dismay,
For as he thought of the loss of his friend,
He pined and wasted away;
A fleeting shadow he became,
And is unto this day.

Now ever since, he has roamed the hills,
And wandered up and down;

Among the rocks and cliffs he hides,
But nowhere makes his home;
For no one will shelter him over night,
And no one will him own.

Whenever friend or foe goes by,
His taunting voice they hear,
And he hoots in derision when they pass,
Or he mocks when they venture near,
For his name it is echo, Bah-swa-way,
Who forsook his friend once dear.

The two fair maidens waited long;
For their lovers to return;
But disappointed, rose on high,
To where the bright stars burn;
And now as morning and evening stars;
These sentinels take their turn.

The pole star's light, in northern sky,
Not always is secure;
The morning star, may hide its light,
The evening, not be sure;
But friendship born of holy love,
Forever will endure.

THROUGH TIME AND BITTER DISTANCE

BY E. PAULINE JOHNSON

Unknown to you, I walk the cheerless shore.
The cutting blast, the hurl of biting brine,
May freeze, and still, and bind the waves at war,
Ere you will ever know, O! Heart of mine,
That I have sought, reflected in the blue
Of these sea depths, some shadow of your eyes;
Have hoped the laughing waves would sing of you,
But this is all my starving sight descries—

I.

Far out at sea a sail
Bends to the freshening breeze,
Yields to the rising gale,
That sweeps the seas;

II.

Yields, as a bird wind-tossed,
To saltish waves that fling
Their spray, whose rime and frost
Like crystals cling

III.

To canvas, mast and spar,
Till, gleaming like a gem,
She sinks beyond the far
Horizon's hem.

IV.

Lost to my longing sight,
And nothing left to me
Save an oncoming night,—
An empty sea.

ALGONQUIN LOVE SONG

BY WILLIAM EDGAR BROWN

O! come my beloved and climb with me,
That shining mountain side —
We'll watch the beautiful sun go down,
And talk of the leaves so sere and brown;
And the day you will be my bride,
Well sit till the beautiful traveler of night
Shines high, o'er the mountain side.

We'll watch the little stars follow their chief,
And the Northern Lights play ball;
The Lightning winking, and lighting her pipe,
We'll list to the Thunder Bird beat with bis
might,
And the Whirlwind race with the Squall.
We will sit till all living creatures sleep;
But well not go to sleep at all.

We will sit on the beautiful mountain, nor mind,
The owl's shrill "Go to sleep all!"
We will watch the stars in their sleepless flight,
As they travel above us the whole of the night,
For they do not mind it at all.
We will sit more closely together, and think,
Of ourselves, and that is all.

Again the "go to sleep" call will be heard,
And the night traveler closer will come,
To warn us that now all are dreaming of Mars,
Excepting ourselves, and the bright little stars,
And the Thunder Bird beats not his drum,

The Lightning ceased winking and smoking her
pipe,
And the Thunder Bird beats not his drum.

Now truly the owl is a wise little bird,

A sage and philosopher he;
And thus, when he sings his quaint "Go to sleep all!"

Each young man, and maiden, should list to his call,
And safe in their own room should be;
Nor e'er be misguided by twinkling stars,
 But list to the owl's earnest plea.

Hopi Katcinas drawn by Kutcahanauu (White-Bear)

THE STAR MAIDEN

BY MARGARET COMPTON

The Ojibways were a great nation whom the fairies loved. Their land was the home of many spirits, and as long as they lived on the shores of the great lakes the woods in that country were full of fairies. Some of them dwelt in the moss at the roots or on the trunks of trees. Others hid beneath the mushrooms and toadstools. Some changed themselves into bright-winged butterflies or tinier insects with shining wings. This they did that they might be near the children they loved and play with them where they could see and be seen.

But there were also evil spirits in the land. These burrowed in the ground, gnawed at the roots of the loveliest flowers and destroyed them. They breathed upon the corn and blighted it. They listened whenever they heard men talking, and carried the news to those with whom it would make most mischief.

It is because of these wicked fairies that the Indian must be silent in the woods and must not whisper confidences in the camp unless he is sure the spirits are fast asleep under the white blanket of the snow.

The Ojibways looked well after the interests of the good spirits. They shielded the flowers and stepped carefully aside when moss or flower was in their path. They brushed no moss from the trees, and they never snared the sunbeams, for on them thousands of fairies came down from the sky. When the chase was over they sat in the doorways of their wigwams smoking, and as they watched the blue circles drift and fade into the darkness of the evening, they listened to the voices of the fairies and the insects' hum and the thousand tiny noises that night always brings.

One night as they were listening they saw a bright light shining in the top of the tallest trees. It was a star brighter than all the others, and it seemed very near the earth. When they went close to the tree they found that it was really caught in the topmost branches.

The wise men of the tribe were summoned and for three nights they sat about the council fire, but they came to no conclusion about the beautiful star. At last one of the young warriors went to them and told them that the truth had come to him in a dream.

While asleep the west wind had lifted the curtains of his wigwam and the light of the star fell full upon him. Suddenly a beautiful maiden stood at his side. She smiled upon him, and as he gazed speechless she told him that her home was in the star and that in wandering over all the earth she had seen no land so fair as the land of the Ojibways. Its flowers, its sweet-voiced birds, its rivers, its beautiful lakes, the mountains clothed in green, these had charmed her, and she wished to be no more a wanderer. If they would welcome her she would make her home among them, and she asked them to choose a place in which she might dwell.

The council were greatly pleased; but they could not agree upon what was best to offer the Star Maiden, so they decided to ask her to choose for herself.

She searched first among the flowers of the prairie. There she found the fairies' ring, where the little spirits danced on moonlight nights. "Here," thought she, "I will rest." But as she swung herself backwards and forwards on the stem of a lovely blossom, she heard a terrible noise and fled in great fear. A vast herd of buffaloes came and took possession of the fairies' ring, where they rolled over one another, and bellowed so they could be heard far on the trail. No gentle star maiden could choose such a resting-place.

She next sought the mountain rose. It was cool and pleasant, the moss was soft to her dainty feet, and she could talk to the spirits she loved, whose homes were in the stars. But the mountain was steep, and huge rocks hid from her view the nation that she loved.

She was almost in despair, when one day as she looked down from the edge of the wild rose leaf she saw a white flower with a heart of gold shining on the waters of the lake below her.

40

As she looked a canoe steered by the young warrior who had told her wishes to his people, shot past, and his strong, brown hand brushed the edge of the flower.

"That is the home for me," she cried, and half-skipping, half-flying down the side of the mountain, she quickly made her way to the flower and hid herself in its bosom. There she could watch the stars as well as when she looked upward from the cup of the mountain rose; there she could talk to the star spirits, for they bathed in the clear lake; and best of all, there she could watch the people whom she loved, for their canoes were always upon the water.

MY INDIAN GRANDMOTHER

BY OHIYESA (CHARLES A. EASTMAN)

As a motherless child, I always regarded my good grandmother as the wisest of guides and the best of protectors. It was not long before I began to realize her superiority to most of her contemporaries. This idea was not gained entirely from my own observation, but also from a knowledge of the high regard in which she was held by other women. Aside from her native talent and ingenuity, she was endowed with a truly wonderful memory. No other midwife in her day and tribe could compete with her in skill and judgment. Her observations in practice were all preserved in her mind for reference, as systematically as if they had been written upon the pages of a notebook.

I distinctly recall one occasion when she took me with her into the woods in search of certain medicinal roots.

"Why do you not use all kinds of roots for medicines?" said I.

"Because," she replied, in her quick, characteristic manner, "the Great Mystery does not will us to find things too easily. In that case everybody would be a medicine-giver, and Ohiyesa must learn that there are many secrets which the Great Mystery will disclose only to the most worthy. Only those who seek him fasting and in solitude will receive his signs."

With this and many similar explanations she wrought in my soul wonderful and lively conceptions of the "Great Mystery" and of the effects of prayer and solitude. I continued my childish questioning.

"But why did you not dig those plants that we saw in the woods, of the same kind that you are digging now?"

"For the same reason that we do not like the berries we find in the shadow of deep woods as well as the ones which grow in sunny places. The latter have more sweetness and flavor. Those herbs which have medicinal virtues should be sought in a place that is neither too wet nor too dry, and where they have a

43

generous amount of sunshine to maintain their vigor.

"Some day Ohiyesa will be old enough to know the secrets of medicine; then I will tell him all. But if you should grow up to be a bad man, I must withhold these treasures from you and give them to your brother, for a medicine man must be a good and wise man. I hope Ohiyesa will be a great medicine man when he grows up. To be a great warrior is a noble ambition; but to be a mighty medicine man is a nobler!"

She said these things so thoughtfully and impressively that I cannot but feel and remember them even to this day.]

Our native women gathered all the wild rice, roots, berries and fruits which formed an important part of our food. This was distinctively a woman's work. Uncheedah (grandmother) understood these matters perfectly, and it became a kind of instinct with her to know just where to look for each edible variety and at what season of the year. This sort of labor gave the Indian women every opportunity to observe and study Nature after their fashion; and in this Uncheedah was more acute than most of the men. The abilities of her boys were not all inherited from their father; indeed, the stronger family traits came obviously from her. She was a leader among the native women, and they came to her, not only for medical aid, but for advice in all their affairs.

In bravery she equaled any of the men. This trait, together with her ingenuity and alertness of mind, more than once saved her and her people from destruction. Once, when we were roaming over a region occupied by other tribes, and on a day when most of the men were out upon the hunt, a party of hostile Indians suddenly appeared. Although there were a few men left at home, they were taken by surprise at first and scarcely knew what to do, when this woman came forward and advanced alone to meet our foes. She had gone some distance when some of the men followed her. She met the strangers and offered her hand to them. They accepted her friendly greeting; and as a result of her brave act we were left unmolested and at peace.

Another story of her was related to me by my father. My grandfather, who was a noted hunter, often wandered away from his band in search of game. In this instance he had with him only his own family of three boys and his wife. One evening, when he returned from the chase, he found to his surprise that she had built a stockade around her teepee.

She had discovered the danger-sign in a single foot-print, which she saw at a glance was not that of her husband, and she was also convinced that it was not the foot-print of a Sioux, from the shape of the moccasin. This ability to recognize footprints is general among the Indians, but more marked in certain individuals.

This courageous woman had driven away a party of five Ojibway warriors. They approached the lodge cautiously, but her dog gave timely warning, and she poured into them from behind her defences the contents of a double-barrelled gun, with such good effect that the astonished braves thought it wise to retreat.

I was not more than five or six years old when the Indian soldiers came one day and destroyed our large buffalo-skin teepee. It was charged that my uncle had hunted alone a large herd of buffaloes. This was not exactly true. He had unfortunately frightened a large herd while shooting a deer in the edge of the woods. However, it was customary to punish such an act severely, even though the offense was accidental.

When we were attacked by the police, I was playing in the teepee, and the only other person at home was Uncheedah. I had not noticed their approach, and when the war-cry was given by thirty or forty Indians with strong lungs, I thought my little world was coming to an end. Instantly innumerable knives and tomahawks penetrated our frail home, while bullets went through the poles and tent-fastenings up above our heads.

I hardly know what I did, but I imagine it was just what any other little fellow would have done under like circumstances. My first clear realization of the situation was when Uncheedah had a dispute with the leader, claiming that the matter had not been properly investigated, and that none of the policemen had attained to a reputation in war which would justify them in touching her son's teepee. But alas! our poor dwelling was already an unrecognizable ruin; even the poles were broken into splinters.

The Indian women, after reaching middle age, are usually heavy and lack agility, but my grandmother was in this also an exception. She was fully sixty when I was born; and when I was seven years old she swam across a swift and wide stream, carrying me on her back, because she did not wish to expose me to accident in one of the clumsy round boats of bull-hide which were rigged up to cross the rivers which impeded our way, especially in the springtime. Her strength and endurance were remarkable. Even after she had attained the age of eighty-two, she one day walked twenty-five miles without appearing much fatigued.

I marvel now at the purity and elevated sentiment possessed by this woman, when I consider the customs and habits of her people at the time. When her husband died she was still comparatively a young woman—still active, clever and industrious. She was descended from a haughty chieftain of the "Dwellers among the Leaves." Although women of her age and position were held to be eligible to re-marriage, and she had several persistent suitors who were men of her own age and chiefs, yet she preferred to cherish in solitude the memory of her husband.

I was very small when my uncle brought home two Ojibway young women. In the fight in which they were captured, none of the Sioux war party had been killed; therefore they were sympathized with and tenderly treated by the Sioux women. They were apparently happy, although of course they felt deeply the losses sustained at the time of their capture, and they did not fail to show their appreciation of the kindnesses received at our hands.

As I recall now the remarks made by one of them at the time of their final release, they appear to me quite remarkable. They lived in my grandmother's family for two years, and were then returned to their people at a great peace council of the two nations. When they were about to leave my grandmother, the elder of the two sisters first embraced her, and then spoke somewhat as follows:

"You are a brave woman and a true mother. I understand now why your son so bravely conquered our band, and took my sister and myself captive. I hated him at first, but now I admire him, because he did just what my father, my brother or my husband would have done had they opportunity. He did even more. He saved us from the tomahawks of his fellow-warriors, and brought us to his home to know a noble and a brave woman.

"I shall never forget your many favors shown to us. But I must go. I belong to my tribe and I shall return to them. I will endeavor to be a true woman also, and to teach my boys to be generous warriors like your son."

Her sister chose to remain among the Sioux all her life, and she married one of our young men.

"I shall make the Sioux and the Ojibways," she said, "to be as brothers."

There are many other instances of intermarriage with captive women. The mother of the well-known Sioux chieftain, Wabashaw, was an Ojibway woman. I once knew a woman who was said to be a white captive. She was married to a noted warrior, and had a fine family of five boys. She was well accustomed to the Indian ways, and as a child I should not have suspected that she was white. The skins of these people became so sunburned and full of paint that it required a keen eye to distinguish them from the real Indians.

Three Winnebago women, one with child on her back, on hillside possibly photographed by C. L. Hamilton

THE MOTHER OF THE WORLD

A TRADITION OF THE DOG-RIBS.

BY JAMES ATHEARN JONES

In the frozen regions of the North, beyond the lands which are now the hunting-grounds of the Snakes and Coppermines, there lived, when no other being but herself was, a woman who became the mother of the world. She was a little woman, our fathers told us, not taller than the shoulders of a young maiden of our nation, but she was very beautiful and very wise. Whether she was good-tempered or cross, I cannot tell, for she had no husband, and so there was nothing to vex her, or to try her patience. She had not, as the women of our nation now have, to pound corn, or to fetch home heavy loads of buffalo flesh, or to make snow-sledges, or to wade into the icy rivers to spear salmon, or basket kepling, or to lie concealed among the wet marsh grass and wild rice to snare pelicans, and cranes, and goosanders, while her lazy, good-for-nothing husband lay at home, smoking his pipe, and drinking the pleasant juice of the Nishcaminnick by the warm fire in his cabin. She had only to procure her own food, and this was the berries, and hips, and sorrel, and rock-moss, which, being found plentifully near her cave, were plucked with little trouble. Of these she gathered, in their season, when the sun beamed on the earth like a maiden that loves and is beloved, a great deal to serve her for food when the snows hid the earth from her sight, and the cold winds from the fields of eternal frost obliged her to remain in her rude cavern. Though alone, she was happy. In the summer it was her amusement to watch the juniper and the alders, as they put forth, first their leaves, and then their buds, and when the latter became blossoms, promising to supply the fruit she loved, her observation became more curious and her feelings more interested; then would her heart beat with the rapture of a young mother, whose gaze is fixed on her sleeping child, and her eyes glisten with the dew of joy which wets the cheeks of those who meet long parted friends. Then she would wander forth to search for the little ber-

51

ry whose flower is yellow, and which requires keen eyes to find it in its hiding-place in the grass, and the larger which our white brother eats with his buffalo-meat; and their progress, from the putting forth of the leaf to the ripening of the fruit, was watched by her with eager joy. When tired of gazing upon the pine and stunted poplar, she would lie down in the shade of the creeping birch and dwarf willow, and sink to rest, and dream dreams which were not tinged with the darkness of evil. The sighing of the wind through the branches of the trees, and the murmur of little streams through the thicket, were her music. Throughout the land there was nothing to hurt her, or make her afraid, for there was nothing in it that had life, save herself and the little flower which blooms among thorns. And these two dwelt together like sisters.

One day, when the mother of the world was out gathering berries, and watching the growth of a young pine, which had sprung up near her friend the flower, and threatened, as the flower said, "to take away the beams of the sun from it," she was scared by the sight of a strange creature, which ran upon four legs, and to all her questions answered nothing but "Bow, wow, wow." To every question our mother asked, the creature made the same answer, "bow, wow, wow." So she left off asking him questions, for they were sure to be replied to in three words of a language she could not understand. Did he ask for berries? no, for she offered him a handful of the largest and juiciest which grew in the valley, and he neither took them nor thanked her, unless "bow" meant "thank you." Was he admiring the tall young pines, or the beautiful blossoms of the cranberry, or the graceful bend of the willow, and asking her to join him in his admiration? She knew not, and leaving him to his thoughts, and to utter his strange words with none to reply, she returned to her cave.

Scarcely was she seated on her bed of dried leaves when he came in, and, wagging his tail, and muttering as before, lay down at her feet. Occasionally he would look up into her face very kindly, and then drop his head upon his paws. By and by he was fast asleep, and our mother, who had done no evil action, the remembrance of which should keep her awake, who never stole a beaver-trap, or told a lie, or laughed at a priest, was very soon in the same condition. Then the Manitou of Dreams came to her, and she saw strange things in her sleep. She dreamed that it wan night, and the sun had sunk behind the high and broken hills which lay beyond the valley of her dwelling, that the dwarf willow bowed its graceful head still lower with the weight of its tears, which are the evening dew, and the dandelion again imprisoned its leaves within its veil of brown. So far her dreams so closely resembled the reality, that for a time she thought she was awake, and that it was her own world—her cave, her berries, and her flowers, which were before her vision. But an object speedily came to inform her that she dwelt in the paradise of dreams—in the land of departed ideas. At the foot of her couch of leaves, in the place of the dog which she had left there when she slept, stood a being somewhat resembling that she had beheld in the warm season, when bending over the river to lave her bosom with the cooling fluid. It was taller than herself, and there was something on its brow which proclaimed it to be fiercer and bolder, formed to wrestle with rough winds, and to laugh at the coming tempests. For the first time since she was, she turned away to tremble, her soul filled with a new and undefinable feeling, for which she could not account. After shading her eyes a moment from the vision, she looked again, and though her trembling increased, and her brain became giddy, she did not wish the being away, nor did she motion it to go. Why should she? There was a smile upon its lip and brow, and a softness diffused over every feature, which gradually restored her confidence, and gave her the assurance that it would not harm her. She dreamed that the creature came to her arms, and she thought that it passed the season of darkness with its cheek laid on her bosom. To her imagination, the breath which it breathed on her lips was balmy as the juice of the Sweet Gum Tree, or the dew from her little neighbour, the flower. When it spoke, though she could not understand its language, her heart heaved more tumultuously, she knew not why, and when it ceased speaking, her sighs came thick

53

till it spoke again. When she awoke it was gone, the beams of the star of day shone through the fissures of her cavern, and, in the place of the beautiful and loved being lay the strange creature, with the four legs and the old "bow, wow, wow."

Four moons passed, and brought no change of scene to the mother of the world. By night, her dreams were ever the same: there was always the same dear and beloved being, each day dearer and more beloved, coming with the shades, and departing with the sun, folding her in its arms, breathing balm on her lips, and pressing her bosom with its downy cheek. By day, the dog was always at her side, whether she went to gather berries or cresses, or to bathe her limbs in the stream. Whenever the dog was there, the more beloved being was not; when night came, the dog as surely disappeared, and the other, seen in dreams, supplied his place. But she herself became changed. She took no more joy in the scenes which once pleased her. The pines she had planted throve unnoticed; the creeping birch stifled the willow and the juniper, and she heeded it not; the sweetest berries grew tasteless—she even forgot to visit her pretty sister, the rose. Yet she knew not the cause of her sudden change, nor of the anxiety and apprehension which filled her mind. Why tears bedewed her cheeks till her eyes became blind, why she trembled at times, and grew sick, and feinted, and fell to the earth, she knew not. Her feelings told her of a change, but the relation of its cause, the naming to her startled ear of the mystery of "the dog by day, and the man by night," was reserved for a being, who was to prepare the world for the reception of the mighty numbers which were to be the progeny of its mother.

She had wandered forth to a lonely valley—lonely where all was lonely—to weep and sigh over her lost peace, and to think of the dear being with which that loss seemed to her to be in some way connected, when suddenly the sky became darkened, and she saw the form of a being shaped like that which visited her in her sleep, but of immense proportions, coming towards her from the east. The clouds wreathed themselves around his head, his hair swept the mists from the mountain-tops, his eyes were larger than the rising sun when he wears the red flush of anger in the Frog-Moon, and his voice, when he gave it full tone, was louder than the thunder of the Spirit's Bay of Lake Huron. But to the woman he spoke in soft whispers; his terrific accents were reserved for the dog, who quailed beneath them in evident terror. not daring even to utter his only words, "bow, wow." The mother of the world related to him her dreams, and asked him why, since she had had them, she was so changed—why she now found no joy in the scenes which once pleased her, but rather wished that she no longer was, her dreams being now all that she loved. The mighty being told her that they were not dreams, but a reality; that the dog which now stood by her side was invested by the Master of Life with power to quit, at the coming in of the shades, the shape of a dog, and to take that of MAN, a being who was the counterpart of herself, but formed with strength and resolution, to counteract, by wisdom and sagacity, and to overcome, by strength and valour, the rough difficulties and embarrassments which were to spring up in the path of human life; that he was to be fierce and bold, and she gentle and afraid. He told her that the change she complained of, and which had given her so much grief, wetted her cheek with tears, and filled her bosom with sighs, was the natural result of the intimate connection of two such beings, and was the mode of perpetuating the human race, which had been decreed by the Master of Life; that before the buds now forming should be matured to fruit, she would give birth to two helpless little beings, whom she must feed with her milk, and rear with tender care, for from them would the world be peopled. He had been sent, he said, by the Good Spirit to level and prepare the earth for the reception of the race who were to inhabit it.

Hitherto the world had lain a rude and shapeless mass—the great, man now reduced it to order. He threw the rough and stony crags into the deep valleys—he moved the frozen mountain to fill up the boiling chasm. When he had levelled the earth, which before was a thing without form, he marked out with his great walking-staff the lakes, ponds, and rivers, and caused them

55

to be filled with water from the interior of the earth, bidding them to be replenished from the rains and melted snows which should fall from the skies, till they should be no more.

When he had prepared the earth for the residence of the beings who were to people it, he caught the dog, and, notwithstanding the cries of the mother of the world, and her entreaties to him to spare its life, he tore it in pieces, and distributed it over the earth, and the water, and into air. The entrails he threw into the lakes, ponds, and rivers, commanding them to become fish, and they became fish. These waters, in which no living creature before moved, were now filled with salmon, trout, pike, tittymeg, methy, barble, turbot, and tench, while along the curling waves of the Great Lake the mighty black and white whale, the more sluggish porpoise, and many other finny creatures, sported their gambols. The flesh he dispersed over the land, commanding it to become different kinds of beasts and land-animals, and it obeyed his commands. The heavy moose, and the stupid we-was-kish, came to drink in the Coppermine with the musk-ox, and the deer, and the buffalo. The quiquehatch, and his younger brother, the black bear, and the wolf, that cooks his meat without fire, and the cunning fox, and the wild cat, and the wolverine, were all from the flesh of the dog. The otter was the tail of the dog, the wejack was one of his fore-paws, and the horned horse, and the walrus, were his nose.

Nor did the great man omit to make the skin furnish its proportion of the tribes of living beings. He tore it into many small pieces, and threw it into the air, commanding it to become the different tribes of fowls and birds, and it became the different tribes of fowls and birds. Then first was seen the mighty bird which builds its nest on trees which none can climb, and in the crevices of inaccessible rocks—the eagle, which furnishes the Indians with feathers to their arrows, and steals away the muskrat and the young beaver as his recompense. Then was the sacred falcon first seen winging his way to the land of long winters; and the bird of alarm, the cunning old owl, and his sister's little son, the cob-a-de-cooch, and the ho-ho. All the birds which skim through the air, or plunge into the water, were formed from the skin of the dog.

When the great man had thus filled the earth with living creatures, he called the mother of the world to him, and gave to her and her offspring the things which he had created, with full power to kill, eat, and never to spare, telling her that he had commanded them to multiply for her use in abundance. When he had finished speaking, he returned to the place whence he came, and has never been heard of since. In due time, the mother of the world was delivered of two children, a son and a daughter, both having the dark visage of the Indian race, and from them proceeded the Dog-ribs, and all the other nations of the earth. The white men were from the same source, but the father of them, having once upon a time been caught stealing a beaver-trap, he become so terrified that he lost his original colour and never regained it, and his children remain with the same pale cheeks to this day.

Brothers, I have told you no lie.

HIAWATHA'S WOOING

BY HENRY W. LONGFELLOW

"As unto the bow the cord is,
So unto the man is woman;
Though she bends him, she obeys him,
Though she draws him, yet she follows;
Useless each without the other!"

Thus the youthful Hiawatha
Said within himself and pondered,
Much perplexed by various feelings,
Listless, longing, hoping, fearing,
Dreaming still of Minnehaha,
Of the lovely Laughing Water,
In the land of the Dacotahs.

"Wed a maiden of your people,"
Warning said the old Nokomis;
"Go not eastward, go not westward,
For a stranger, whom we know not!
Like a fire upon the hearth-stone
Is a neighbor's homely daughter,
Like the starlight or the moonlight
Is the handsomest of strangers!"

Thus dissuading spoke Nokomis,
And my Hiawatha answered
Only this: "Dear old Nokomis,
Very pleasant is the firelight,
But I like the starlight better,
Better do I like the moonlight!"

Gravely then said old Nokomis:
"Bring not here an idle maiden,

Bring not here a useless woman,
Hands unskillful, feet unwilling;
Bring a wife with nimble fingers,
Heart and hand that move together,
Feet that run on willing errands!"

Smiling answered Hiawatha:
"In the land of the Dacotahs
Lives the Arrow-maker's daughter,
Minnehaha, Laughing Water,
Handsomest of all the women.
I will bring her to your wigwam,
She shall run upon your errands,
Be your starlight, moonlight, firelight,
Be the sunlight of my people!"

Still dissuading said Nokomis:
"Bring not to my lodge a stranger
From the land of the Dacotahs!
Very fierce are the Dacotahs,
Often is there war between us,
There are feuds yet unforgotten,
Wounds that ache and still may open!"

Laughing answered Hiawatha:
"For that reason, if no other,
Would I wed the fair Dacotah,
That our tribes might be united,
That old feuds might be forgotten,
And old wounds be healed forever!"

Thus departed Hiawatha
To the land of the Dacotahs,
To the land of handsome women;
Striding over moor and meadow,
Through interminable forests,

Through uninterrupted silence.

With his moccasins of magic,
At each stride a mile he measured;
Yet the way seemed long before him,
And his heart outran his footsteps;
And he journeyed without resting,
Till he heard the cataract's laughter,
Heard the Falls of Minnehaha
Calling to him through the silence.
"Pleasant is the sound!" he murmured,
"Pleasant is the voice that calls me!"

On the outskirts of the forests,
'Twixt the shadow and the sunshine,
Herds of fallow deer were feeding,
But they saw not Hiawatha;
To his bow he whispered, "Fail not!"
To his arrow whispered, "Swerve not!"
Sent it singing on its errand,
To the red heart of the roebuck;
Threw the deer across his shoulder,
And sped forward without pausing.

At the doorway of his wigwam
Sat the ancient Arrow-maker,
In the land of the Dacotahs,
Making arrow-heads of jasper,
Arrow-heads of chalcedony.
At his side, in all her beauty,
Sat the lovely Minnehaha,
Sat his daughter, Laughing Water,

Plaiting mats of flags and rushes
Of the past the old man's thoughts were,
And the maiden's of the future.

He was thinking, as he sat there,
Of the days when with such arrows
He had struck the deer and bison,
On the Muskoday, the meadow;
Shot the wild goose, flying southward
On the wing, the clamorous Wawa;
Thinking of the great war-parties,
How they came to buy his arrows,
Could not fight without his arrows.
Ah, no more such noble warriors
Could be found on earth as they were!
Now the men were all like women,
Only used their tongues for weapons!

She was thinking of a hunter,
From another tribe and country,
Young and tall and very handsome,
Who one morning, in the Spring-time,
Came to buy her father's arrows,
Sat and rested in the wigwam,
Lingered long about the doorway,
Looking back as he departed.
She had heard her father praise him,
Praise his courage and his wisdom;
Would he come again for arrows
To the Falls of Minnehaha?
On the mat her hands lay idle,
And her eyes were very dreamy.

Through their thoughts they heard a footstep,
Heard a rustling in the branches,
And with glowing cheek and forehead,
With the deer upon his shoulders,
Suddenly from out the woodlands
Hiawatha stood before them.

Straight the ancient Arrow-maker
Looked up gravely from his labor,
Laid aside the unfinished arrow,
Bade him enter at the doorway,
Saying, as he rose to meet him,
"Hiawatha, you are welcome!"

At the feet of Laughing Water
Hiawatha laid his burden,
Threw the red deer from his shoulders;
And the maiden looked up at him,
Looked up from her mat of rushes,
Said with gentle look and accent,
"You are welcome, Hiawatha!"

Very spacious was the wigwam,
Made of deer-skins dressed and whitened,
With the Gods of the Dacotahs
Drawn and painted on its curtains,
And so tall the doorway, hardly
Hiawatha stooped to enter,
Hardly touched his eagle-feathers
As he entered at the doorway.

Then uprose the Laughing Water,
From the ground fair Minnehaha,
Laid aside her mat unfinished,
Brought forth food and set before them,
Water brought them from the brooklet,
Gave them food in earthen vessels,
Gave them drink in bowls of bass-wood,
Listened while the guest was speaking,
Listened while her father answered,
But not once her lips she opened,
Not a single word she uttered.

Yes, as in a dream she listened
To the words of Hiawatha,
As he talked of old Nokomis,
Who had nursed him in his childhood,
As he told of his companions,
Chibiabos, the musician,
And the very strong man, Kwasind,
And of happiness and plenty
In the land of the Ojibways,
In the pleasant land and peaceful.

"After many years of warfare,
Many years of strife and bloodshed,
There is peace between the Ojibways
And the tribe of the Dacotahs."
Thus continued Hiawatha,
And then added, speaking slowly,
"That this peace may last forever,
And our hands be clasped more closely,
And our hearts be more united,
Give me as my wife this maiden,
Minnehaha, Laughing Water,
Loveliest of Dacotah women!"

And the ancient Arrow-maker
Paused a moment ere he answered,
Smoked a little while in silence,
Looked at Hiawatha proudly,
Fondly looked at Laughing Water,
And made answer very gravely:
"Yes, if Minnehaha wishes;
Let your heart speak, Minnehaha!"

And the lovely Laughing Water
Seemed more lovely as she stood there,
Neither willing nor reluctant,

As she went to Hiawatha,
Softly took the seat beside him,
While she said, and blushed to say it,
"I will follow you, my husband!"

This was Hiawatha's wooing!
Thus it was he won the daughter
Of the ancient Arrow-maker,
In the land of the Dacotahs!

From the wigwam he departed,
Leading with him Laughing Water;
Hand in hand they went together,
Through the woodland and the meadow,
Left the old man standing lonely
At the doorway of his wigwam,
Heard the Falls of Minnehaha
Calling to them from the distance,
Crying to them from afar off,
"Fare thee well, O Minnehaha!"

And the ancient Arrow-maker
Turned again unto his labor,
Sat down by his sunny doorway,
Murmuring to himself, and saying:
"Thus it is our daughters leave us,
Those we love, and those who love us!
Just when they have learned to help us,
When we are old and lean upon them,
Comes a youth with flaunting feathers,
With his flute of reeds, a stranger
Wanders piping through the village,
Beckons to the fairest maiden,
And she follows where he leads her,
Leaving all things for the stranger!"

Pleasant was the journey homeward,
Through interminable forests,
Over meadow, over mountain,
Over river, hill, and hollow.
Short it seemed to Hiawatha,
Though they journeyed very slowly,
Though his pace he checked and slackened
To the steps of Laughing Water.

Over wide and rushing rivers
In his arms he bore the maiden;
Light he thought her as a feather,
As the plume upon his head-gear;
Cleared the tangled pathway for her,
Bent aside the swaying branches,
Made at night a lodge of branches,
And a bed with boughs of hemlock,
And a fire before the doorway
With the dry cones of the pine-tree.

All the travelling winds went with them,
O'er the meadows, through the forest;
All the stars of night looked at them,
Watched with sleepless eyes their slumber;
From his ambush in the oak-tree
Peeped the squirrel, Adjidaumo,
Watched with eager eyes the lovers;
And the rabbit, the Wabasso,
Scampered from the path before them,
Peering, peeping from his burrow,
Sat erect upon his haunches,
Watched with curious eyes the lovers.

Pleasant was the journey homeward!
All the birds sang loud and sweetly
Songs of happiness and heart's-ease;

Sang the bluebird, the Owaissa,
"Happy are you, Hiawatha,
Having such a wife to love you!"
Sang the robin, the Opechee,
"Happy are you, Laughing Water,
Having such a noble husband!"

From the sky the sun benignant
Looked upon them through the branches,
Saying to them, "O my children,
Love is sunshine, hate is shadow,
Life is checkered shade and sunshine,
Rule by love, O Hiawatha!"

From the sky the moon looked at them,
Filled the lodge with mystic splendors,
Whispered to them, "O my children,
Day is restless, night is quiet,
Man imperious, woman feeble;
Half is mine, although I follow;
Rule by patience, Laughing Water!"

Thus it was they journeyed homeward;
Thus it was that Hiawatha
To the lodge of old Nokomis
Brought the moonlight, starlight, firelight,
Brought the sunshine of his people,
Minnehaha, Laughing Water,
Handsomest of all the women
In the land of the Dacotahs,
In the land of handsome women.

FIRST IMPRESSIONS OF CIVILIZATION

BY OHIYESA (CHARLES A. EASTMAN)

I was scarcely old enough to know anything definite about the "Big Knives," as we called the white men, when the terrible Minnesota massacre broke up our home and I was carried into exile. I have already told how I was adopted into the family of my father's younger brother, when my father was betrayed and imprisoned. We all supposed that he had shared the fate of those who were executed at Mankato, Minnesota.

Now the savage philosophers looked upon vengeance in the field of battle as a lofty virtue. To avenge the death of a relative or of a dear friend was considered a great deed. My uncle, accordingly, had spared no pains to instill into my young mind the obligation to avenge the death of my father and my older brothers. Already I looked eagerly forward to the day when I should find an opportunity to carry out his teachings. Meanwhile, he himself went upon the war-path and returned with scalps every summer. So it may be imagined how I felt toward the Big Knives!

On the other hand, I had heard marvelous things of this people. In some things we despised them; in others we regarded them as wakan (mysterious), a race whose power bordered upon the supernatural. I learned that they had made a "fire-boat." I could not understand how they could unite two elements which cannot exist together. I thought the water would put out the fire, and the fire would consume the boat if it had the shadow of a chance. This was to me a preposterous thing! But when I was told that the Big Knives had created a "fire-boat-walks-on-mountains" (a locomotive) it was too much to believe.

"Why," declared my informant, "those who saw this monster move said that it flew from mountain to mountain when it seemed to be excited. They said also that they believed it carried a thunder-bird, for they frequently heard his usual war-whoop as the creature sped along!"

Several warriors had observed from a distance one of the first trains on the Northern Pacific, and had gained an exaggerated impression of the wonders of the pale-face. They had seen it go over a bridge that spanned a deep ravine and it seemed to them that it jumped from one bank to the other. I confess that the story almost quenched my ardor and bravery.

Two or three young men were talking together about this fearful invention.

"However," said one, "I understand that this fire-boat-walks-on-mountains cannot move except on the track made for it."

Although a boy is not expected to join in the conversation of his elders, I ventured to ask: "Then it cannot chase us into any rough country?"

"No, it cannot do that," was the reply, which I heard with a great deal of relief.

I had seen guns and various other things brought to us by the French Canadians, so that I had already some notion of the supernatural gifts of the white man; but I had never before heard such tales as I listened to that morning. It was said that they had bridged the Missouri and Mississippi rivers, and that they made immense houses of stone and brick, piled on top of one another until they were as high as high hills. My brain was puzzled with these things for many a day. Finally I asked my uncle why the Great Mystery gave such power to the Washechu (the rich)-sometimes we called them by this name—and not to us Dakotas.

"For the same reason," he answered, "that he gave to Duta the skill to make fine bows and arrows, and to Wachesne no skill to make anything."

"And why do the Big Knives increase so much more in number than the Dakotas?" I continued.

"It has been said, and I think it must be true, that they

have larger families than we do. I went into the house of an Eashecha (a German), and I counted no less than nine children. The eldest of them could not have been over fifteen. When my grandfather first visited them, down at the mouth of the Mississippi, they were comparatively few; later my father visited their Great Father at Washington, and they had already spread over the whole country."

"Certainly they are a heartless nation. They have made some of their people servants—yes, slaves! We have never believed in keeping slaves, but it seems that these Washechu do! It is our belief that they painted their servants black a long time ago, to tell them from the rest, and now the slaves have children born to them of the same color!

"The greatest object of their lives seems to be to acquire possessions—to be rich. They desire to possess the whole world. For thirty years they were trying to entice us to sell them our land. Finally the outbreak gave them all, and we have been driven away from our beautiful country.

"They are a wonderful people. They have divided the day into hours, like the moons of the year. In fact, they measure everything. Not one of them would let so much as a turnip go from his field unless he received full value for it. I understand that their great men make a feast and invite many, but when the feast is over the guests are required to pay for what they have eaten before leaving the house. I myself saw at White Cliff (the name given to St. Paul, Minnesota) a man who kept a brass drum and a bell to call people to his table; but when he got them in he would make them pay for the food!

"I am also informed," said my uncle, "but this I hardly believe, that their Great Chief (President) compels every man to pay him for the land he lives upon and all his personal goods—even for his own existence—every year!" (This was his idea of taxation.) "I am sure we could not live under such a law.

"When the outbreak occurred, we thought that our opportunity had come, for we had learned that the Big Knives were fighting among themselves, on account of a dispute over their slaves. It was said that the Great Chief had allowed slaves in one part of the country and not in another, so there was jealousy, and they had to fight it out. We don't know how true this was.

"There were some praying-men who came to us some time before the trouble arose. They observed every seventh day as a holy day. On that day they met in a house that they had built for that purpose, to sing, pray, and speak of their Great Mystery. I was never in one of these meetings. I understand that they had a large book from which they read. By all accounts they were very different from all other white men we have known, for these never observed any such day, and we never knew them to pray, neither did they ever tell us of their Great Mystery.

"In war they have leaders and war-chiefs of different grades. The common warriors are driven forward like a herd of antelopes to face the foe. It is on account of this manner of fighting—from compulsion and not from personal bravery—that we count no coup on them. A lone warrior can do much harm to a large army of them in a bad country."

It was this talk with my uncle that gave me my first clear idea of the white man. I was almost fifteen years old when my uncle presented me with a flint-lock gun. The possession of the "mysterious iron," and the explosive dirt, or "pulverized coal," as it is called, filled me with new thoughts. All the war-songs that I had ever heard from childhood came back to me with their heroes. It seemed as if I were an entirely new being—the boy had become a man!

"I am now old enough," said I to myself, "and I must beg my uncle to take me with him on his next war-path. I shall soon be able to go among the whites whenever I wish, and to avenge the blood of my father and my brothers."

I had already begun to invoke the blessing of the Great Mystery. Scarcely a day passed that I did not offer up some of my game, so that he might not be displeased with me. My people saw very little of me during the day, for in solitude I found the strength I needed. I groped about in the wilderness, and determined to assume my position as a man. My boyish ways were departing, and a sullen dignity and composure was taking their place.

The thought of love did not hinder my ambitions. I had a vague dream of some day courting a pretty maiden, after I had made my reputation, and won the eagle feathers.

One day, when I was away on the daily hunt, two strangers from the United States visited our camp. They had boldly ventured across the northern border. They were Indians, but clad in the white man's garments. It was as well that I was absent with my gun.

My father, accompanied by an Indian guide, after many days' searching had found us at last. He had been imprisoned at Davenport, Iowa, with those who took part in the massacre or in the battles following, and he was taught in prison and converted by the pioneer missionaries, Drs. Williamson and Riggs. He was under sentence of death, but was among the number against whom no direct evidence was found, and who were finally pardoned by President Lincoln.

When he was released, and returned to the new reservation upon the Missouri river, he soon became convinced that life on a government reservation meant physical and moral degradation. Therefore he determined, with several others, to try the white man's way of gaining a livelihood. They accordingly left the agency against the persuasions of the agent, renounced all government assistance, and took land under the United States Homestead law, on the Big Sioux river. After he had made his home there, he desired to seek his lost child. It was then a dangerous undertaking to cross the line, but his Christian love prompted him to do it. He secured a good guide, and found his way in time through the vast wilderness.

As for me, I little dreamed of anything unusual to happen on my return. As I approached our camp with my game on my shoulder, I had not the slightest premonition that I was suddenly to be hurled from my savage life into a life unknown to me hitherto.

When I appeared in sight my father, who had patiently

listened to my uncle's long account of my early life and training, became very much excited. He was eager to embrace the child who, as he had just been informed, made it already the object of his life to avenge his father's blood. The loving father could not remain in the teepee and watch the boy coming, so he started to meet him. My uncle arose to go with his brother to insure his safety.

My face burned with the unusual excitement caused by the sight of a man wearing the Big Knives' clothing and coming toward me with my uncle.

"What does this mean, uncle?"

"My boy, this is your father, my brother, whom we mourned as dead. He has come for you."

My father added: "I am glad that my son is strong and brave. Your brothers have adopted the white man's way; I came for you to learn this new way, too; and I want you to grow up a good man."

He had brought me some civilized clothing, At first, I disliked very much to wear garments made by the people I had hated so bitterly. But the thought that, after all, they had not killed my father and brothers, reconciled me, and I put on the clothes.

In a few days we started for the States. I felt as if I were dead and traveling to the Spirit Land; for now all my old ideas were to give place to new ones, and my life was to be entirely different from that of the past.

Still, I was eager to see some of the wonderful inventions of the white people. When we reached Fort Totten, I gazed about me with lively interest and a quick imagination.

My father had forgotten to tell me that the fire-boat-walks-on-mountains had its track at Jamestown, and might appear at any moment. As I was watering the ponies, a peculiar shrilling noise pealed forth from just beyond the hills. The ponies threw back their heads and listened; then they ran snorting over the prairie. Meanwhile, I too had taken alarm. I leaped on the back of one of the ponies, and dashed off at full speed. It was a clear day; I could not imagine what had caused such an unearthly noise. It seemed as if the world were about to burst in two!

I got upon a hill as the train appeared. "O!" I said to myself, "that is the fire-boat-walkson-mountains that I have heard about!" Then I drove back the ponies.

My father was accustomed every morning to read from his Bible, and sing a stanza of a hymn. I was about very early with my gun for several mornings; but at last he stopped me as I was preparing to go out, and bade me wait.

I listened with much astonishment. The hymn contained the word Jesus. I did not comprehend what this meant; and my father then told me that Jesus was the Son of God who came on earth to save sinners, and that it was because of him that he had sought me. This conversation made a deep impression upon my mind.

Late in the fall we reached the citizen settlement at Flandreau, South Dakota, where my father and some others dwelt among the whites. Here my wild life came to an end, and my school days began.

Big Winnebago Jim photographed by Unknown

PART FOUR
EDITORIAL

THE OMAHA SUNDAY BEE

PART FOUR
AMUSEMENTS

OMAHA, SUNDAY MORNING, SEPTEMBER 29, 1912.

TEN CENTS

Lo The Poor Indian Prospers

Chief, Shouting Orders For Scalp Dance, at Ak-Sar-Ben,
Grins Ironically - Braves Plot Racing Automobile, Picnics
Long Forgotten - But Squaws Still Work While
Corpulent Bucks Loaf and Smoke

EDITOR'S EXPLANATION FOR "LO THE POOR INDIAN PROSPERS" BY PAUL GREER

  This newspaper article is evidence of some of the strong prejudices that many Americans held against Native Americans in the early twentieth century. Greer is criticizing the way that the Omaha tribe is spending the money that the United States government has been giving them for living on the Winnebago reservation. Throughout the article, Greer uses stereotypical words and phrases, such as "Killed No Palefaces" or "Scalp Dance Ordered," to mock the way that the Omaha tribe is choosing to spend their money when he thinks that they would be better off using it in other ways. Even though he makes these criticisms about the different actions the Omaha tribe is choosing to do with their money, Greer doesn't adequately acknowledge the underlying reason for their choices (Greer, 1920).

  The editors chose to include an image of this article to illustrate the negative associations that came with belonging to an Indigenous community. Since the relationship between the United States government and different Indigenous tribes affected how they were perceived by Americans, it was important to share this aspect of Indigenous identity alongside the more positive ones.

LETTER TO HARRIET CONVERSE

BY ELY S. PARKER

Dear Gayaneshaoh,

    The outpouring of your terrific wrath against certain Christian practices, beliefs and propositions for the ameliora- tion and improvement of certain unchristian people who live on reservations where the English language is not spoken, and where "vice and barbarism" are rampant, was duly received yesterday. The Bishop is right in his reference to the remnants of the Six Nations being yet "deplorably subject to individual disability, disadvantages and wrong arising from their tribal condition," in all except the last proposition. The disabilities, disadvantages and wrongs do not result, however, either pri- marily, consequently or ultimately from their tribal condition and native inheritances, but solely, wholly and absolutely from the unchristian treatment they have always received from Christian white people who speak the English language, who read the English Bible and who are Pharisaically divested of all the elements of vice and barbarism. The tenacity with which the remnants of this people have adhered to their tribal organi- zations and religious traditions is all that has saved them thus far from inevitable extinguishment. When they abandon their birthright for a mess of Christian pottage they will then cease to be a distinctive people. It is useless though to discuss this question, already prejudiced and predetermined by a granit- ic Christian hierarchy from whose judgments and decisions there seems to be no appeal. . . .

Dear Gayaneshaoh,

    On reading your last note I was greatly amused, – and why? Because what I have written heretofore has been tak- en literatim et verbatim and a character given me to which I

81

am no more entitled than the man in the moon! I am credited or charged with being "great," "powerful" and finally crowned as "good"! Oh, my guardian genius, why should I be so burdened with what I am not now and never expect to be! Oh, indeed, would that I could feel a "kindling touch from that pure flame" which a fair and ministering angel would endow me with in the exuberance of prejudiced enthusiasm, and which compels me to sit in sackcloth and ashes. . . .

And why all this commotion of the spirit? Because I am an ideal or a myth and not my real self. I have lost my identity and I look about me in vain for my original being. I never was "great" and never expect to be. I never was "powerful" and would not know how to exercise power were it placed in my hands for use. And that I am "good" or ever dreamed of attaining that blissful condition of being is simply absurd. . . .

All my life I have occupied a false position. As a youth my people voted me a genius and loudly proclaimed that Hawenneyo had destined me to be their savior and gave public thanksgiving for the great blessing they believed had been given them, for unfortunately just at this period they were engaged in an almost endless and nearly hopeless litigated contest for their New York homes and consequently for their very existence.

For many years I was a constant visitor at the State and Federal capitals either seeking legislative relief or in attendance at State and Federal courts. Being only a mere lad, the pale-faced officials with whom I came in contact flattered me and declared that one so young must be extraordinarily endowed to be charged with the conduct of such weighty affairs. I pleased my people in eventually bringing their troubles to a successful and satisfactory termination. I prepared and had approved by the proper authorities a code of laws and rules for the conduct of affairs among themselves and settled them for all time or, for so long as Hawenneyo should let them live.

They saw all this and that it was good. They no longer wanted me nor gave me credit for what had been done. A generation had passed and another grown up since I began to work for them. The young men were confident of their own strength and abilities and needed not the brawny arm of experience to fight their battles for them, nor the wisdom brought about by years of training to guide them any longer. The War of the Rebellion had broken out among the pale-faces, a terrible contest between the slaveholding and non-slaveholding sections of the United States. I had, through the Hon. Wm. H. Seward, personally tendered my services for the non-slaveholding interest. Mr. Seward in short said to me that the struggle in which I wished to assist, was an affair between white men and one in which the Indian was not called on to act. "The fight must be made and settled by the white men alone," he said. "Go home, cultivate your farm, and we will settle our own troubles without any Indian aid."

I did go home and planted crops and myself on the farm, sometimes not leaving it for four and six weeks at a time. But the quarrel of the whites was not so easily or quickly settled. It was not a wrangle of boys, but a struggle of giants and the country was being racked to its very foundations.

Then came to me in my forest home a paper bearing the great red seal of the War Department at Washington. It was an officer's commission in the Army of the United States. The young Indian community had settled in their untutored minds that because I had settled quietly, willingly and unconcernedly in the earning of my living by the sweat of my brow, I was not, therefore, a genius or a man of mind. That they were in truth correct, they did not know, jealousy and envy having prompted the idea and utterance. But now this paper coming from the great Government at Washington offering to confer honors for which I had not served an apprenticeship, nor even asked for, revived among the poor Indians the idea that I was after all a genius and great and powerful, though to them not perceptible. They pleaded with me not to leave them, but to remain as their counsellor, adviser and chief, and that they would be powerless and lost without my presence. They tacitly acknowledged my genius, greatness, and power, and which I did not. When I explained that I was going into the war with a splendid protest of sacrificing my life, as much for their food as for the maintenance of the principles of the Constitution and laws of the United States, and upholding the Union flag in its purity, honor and supremacy over this whole country, they silently and wisely bowed their heads and wept in assent as to the inevitable. I bade them farewell, commended them to the care and protection of Hawenneyo and left them, never expecting to return.

I went from the East to the West and from the West to the East again. They heard of me in great battles and they knew of my association with the great commander of all the Union armies and how I upheld the right arm of his strength, and they said, "How great and powerful is our chief!"

The quarrel between the white men ended and the great commander with his military family settled in Washington, where the great council fire of his nation was annually lighted and blazed in all its glory and fury. As an humble member of this military family I was the envy of many pale-faced subordinate embryo generals who said in whispers, "Parker must be a genius, he is so great and powerful."

In a few years my military chieftain was made head and front of the whole American people, and in his partiality he placed me at the head of the management of the Indian Affairs of the United States. I was myself an Indian and presumably understood them, their wants and the manipulation of their affairs generally. Then, again went out among the whites and Indians the words, "Parker must be a genius, he is so great and powerful." The Indians were universally pleased, and they all were willing to be quiet and remain at peace, and were even asking to be taught civilization and Christianity. I stopped and put an end to all wars either among themselves or with their white brothers, and I sent professed Christian teachers among them. But these things did not suit that class of whites who waxed rich and fat from the plundering of the poor Indians, nor were there teacherships enough to give places to all the hungry and impecunious Christians. Then was the cry raised by all who believed themselves injured or unprovided for: "Nay! this Parker is an Indian genius; he is grown too great and powerful; he doth injure our business and taketh the bread from the mouths of our families and the money from out of our pockets, now, therefore, let us write and put him out of power, so that we may feast as heretofore."

They made their onslaught on my poor innocent head and made the air foul with their malicious and poisonous accusations. They were defeated, but it was no longer a pleasure to discharge patriotic duties in the face of foul slander and abuse. I gave up a thankless position to enjoy my declining days in peace and quiet. But my days are not all peace and quiet. I am pursued by a still small voice constantly echoing, "Thou art a genius, great and powerful," and even my little cousin, the restless Snipe,10 has with her strong, piping voice echoed the refrain, "Thou art great, powerful and good." . . .

Your cousin,
Donehogawa, The Wolf

Winnebago camp scene possibly photographed by C.L.
Hamilton

THE SCHOOL DAYS OF AN
INDIAN GIRL

BY ZITKALA-SA

I.
THE LAND OF RED APPLES.

There were eight in our party of bronzed children who were going East with the missionaries. Among us were three young braves, two tall girls, and we three little ones, Judéwin, Thowin, and I.

We had been very impatient to start on our journey to the Red Apple Country, which, we were told, lay a little beyond the great circular horizon of the Western prairie. Under a sky of rosy apples we dreamt of roaming as freely and happily as we had chased the cloud shadows on the Dakota plains. We had anticipated much pleasure from a ride on the iron horse, but the throngs of staring palefaces disturbed and troubled us.

On the train, fair women, with tottering babies on each arm, stopped their haste and scrutinized the children of absent mothers. Large men, with heavy bundles in their hands, halted near by, and riveted their glassy blue eyes upon us.

I sank deep into the corner of my seat, for I resented being watched. Directly in front of me, children who were no larger than I hung themselves upon the backs of their seats, with their bold white faces toward me. Sometimes they took their forefingers out of their mouths and pointed at my moccasined feet. Their mothers, instead of reproving such rude curiosity, looked closely at me, and attracted their children's further notice to my blanket. This embarrassed me, and kept me constantly on the verge of tears.

I sat perfectly still, with my eyes downcast, daring only now and then to shoot long glances around me. Chancing to turn to the window at my side, I was quite breathless upon seeing one familiar object. It was the telegraph pole which strode by at short paces. Very near my mother's dwelling, along the edge

87

It was very little I could swallow besides my sobs, that evening.

"Oh, I want my mother and my brother Dawée! I want to go to my aunt!" I pleaded; but the ears of the palefaces could not hear me.

From the table we were taken along an upward incline of wooden boxes, which I learned afterward to call a stairway. At the top was a quiet hall, dimly lighted. Many narrow beds were in one straight line down the entire length of the wall. In them lay sleeping brown faces, which peeped just out of the coverings. I was tucked into bed with one of the tall girls, because she talked to me in my mother tongue and seemed to soothe me.

I had arrived in the wonderful land of rosy skies, but I was not happy, as I had thought I should be. My long travel and the bewildering sights had exhausted me. I fell asleep, heaving deep, tired sobs. My tears were left to dry themselves in streaks, because neither my aunt nor my mother was near to wipe them away.

II.

THE CUTTING OF MY LONG HAIR.

The first day in the land of apples was a bitter-cold one; for the snow still covered the ground, and the trees were bare. A large bell rang for breakfast, its loud metallic voice crashing through the belfry overhead and into our sensitive ears. The annoying clatter of shoes on bare floors gave us no peace. The constant clash of harsh noises, with an undercurrent of many voices murmuring an unknown tongue, made a bedlam within which I was securely tied. And though my spirit tore itself in struggling for its lost freedom, all was useless.

A paleface woman, with white hair, came up after us. We were placed in a line of girls who were marching into the dining room. These were Indian girls, in stiff shoes and closely clinging dresses. The small girls wore sleeved aprons and shingled hair. As I walked noiselessly in my soft moccasins, I felt like sinking to the floor, for my blanket had been stripped from of a road thickly bordered with wild sunflowers, some poles like these had been planted by white men. Often I had stopped, on my way down the road, to hold my ear against the pole, and, hearing its low moaning, I used to wonder what the paleface had done to hurt it. Now I sat watching for each pole that glided by to be the last one.

In this way I had forgotten my uncomfortable surroundings, when I heard one of my comrades call out my name. I saw the missionary standing very near, tossing candies and gums into our midst. This amused us all, and we tried to see who could catch the most of the sweetmeats.

Though we rode several days inside of the iron horse, I do not recall a single thing about our luncheons.

It was night when we reached the school grounds. The lights from the windows of the large buildings fell upon some of the icicled trees that stood beneath them. We were led toward an open door, where the brightness of the lights within flooded out over the heads of the excited palefaces who blocked our way. My body trembled more from fear than from the snow I trod upon.

Entering the house, I stood close against the wall. The strong glaring light in the large whitewashed room dazzled my eyes. The noisy hurrying of hard shoes upon a bare wooden floor increased the whirring in my ears. My only safety seemed to be in keeping next to the wall. As I was wondering in which direction to escape from all this confusion, two warm hands grasped me firmly, and in the same moment I was tossed high in midair. A rosy-cheeked paleface woman caught me in her arms. I was both frightened and insulted by such trifling. I stared into her eyes, wishing her to let me stand on my own feet, but she jumped me up and down with increasing enthusiasm. My mother had never made a plaything of her wee daughter. Remembering this I began to cry aloud.

They misunderstood the cause of my tears, and placed me at a white table loaded with food. There our party were united again. As I did not hush my crying, one of the older ones whispered to me, "Wait until you are alone in the night."

my shoulders. I looked hard at the Indian girls, who seemed not to care that they were even more immodestly dressed than I, in their tightly fitting clothes. While we marched in, the boys entered at an opposite door. I watched for the three young braves who came in our party. I spied them in the rear ranks, looking as uncomfortable as I felt. A small bell was tapped, and each of the pupils drew a chair from under the table. Supposing this act meant they were to be seated, I pulled out mine and at once slipped into it from one side. But when I turned my head, I saw that I was the only one seated, and all the rest at our table remained standing. Just as I began to rise, looking shyly around to see how chairs were to be used, a second bell was sounded. All were seated at last, and I had to crawl back into my chair again. I heard a man's voice at one end of the hall, and I looked around to see him. But all the others hung their heads over their plates. As I glanced at the long chain of tables, I caught the eyes of a paleface woman upon me. Immediately I dropped my eyes, wondering why I was so keenly watched by the strange woman. The man ceased his mutterings, and then a third bell was tapped. Every one picked up his knife and fork and began eating. I began crying instead, for by this time I was afraid to venture anything more.

But this eating by formula was not the hardest trial in that first day. Late in the morning, my friend Judéwin gave me a terrible warning. Judéwin knew a few words of English; and she had overheard the paleface woman talk about cutting our long, heavy hair. Our mothers had taught us that only unskilled warriors who were captured had their hair shingled by the enemy. Among our people, short hair was worn by mourners, and shingled hair by cowards!

We discussed our fate some moments, and when Judéwin said, "We have to submit, because they are strong," I rebelled.

"No, I will not submit! I will struggle first!" I answered.

I watched my chance, and when no one noticed, I disappeared. I crept up the stairs as quietly as I could in my squeaking shoes,—my moccasins had been exchanged for shoes. Along the hall I passed, without knowing whither I was going. Turning aside to an open door, I found a large room with three white beds in it. The windows were covered with dark green curtains, which made the room very dim. Thankful that no one was there, I directed my steps toward the corner farthest from the door. On my hands and knees I crawled under the bed, and cuddled myself in the dark corner.

From my hiding place I peered out, shuddering with fear whenever I heard footsteps near by. Though in the hall loud voices were calling my name, and I knew that even Judéwin was searching for me, I did not open my mouth to answer. Then the steps were quickened and the voices became excited. The sounds came nearer and nearer. Women and girls entered the room. I held my breath and watched them open closet doors and peep behind large trunks. Some one threw up the curtains, and the room was filled with sudden light. What caused them to stoop and look under the bed I do not know. I remember being dragged out, though I resisted by kicking and scratching wildly. In spite of myself, I was carried downstairs and tied fast in a chair.

I cried aloud, shaking my head all the while until I felt the cold blades of the scissors against my neck, and heard them gnaw off one of my thick braids. Then I lost my spirit. Since the day I was taken from my mother I had suffered extreme indignities. People had stared at me. I had been tossed about in the air like a wooden puppet. And now my long hair was shingled like a coward's! In my anguish I moaned for my mother, but no one came to comfort me. Not a soul reasoned quietly with me, as my own mother used to do; for now I was only one of many little animals driven by a herder.

III.
THE SNOW EPISODE.

A short time after our arrival we three Dakotas were playing in the snowdrift. We were all still deaf to the English

91

language, excepting Judéwin, who always heard such puzzling things. One morning we learned through her ears that we were forbidden to fall lengthwise in the snow, as we had been doing, to see our own impressions. However, before many hours we had forgotten the order, and were having great sport in the snow, when a shrill voice called us. Looking up, we saw an imperative hand beckoning us into the house. We shook the snow off ourselves, and started toward the woman as slowly as we dared.

Judéwin said: "Now the paleface is angry with us. She is going to punish us for falling into the snow. If she looks straight into your eyes and talks loudly, you must wait until she stops. Then, after a tiny pause, say, 'No.'" The rest of the way we practiced upon the little word "no."

As it happened, Thowin was summoned to judgment first. The door shut behind her with a click.

Judéwin and I stood silently listening at the keyhole. The paleface woman talked in very severe tones. Her words fell from her lips like crackling embers, and her inflection ran up like the small end of a switch. I understood her voice better than the things she was saying. I was certain we had made her very impatient with us. Judéwin heard enough of the words to realize all too late that she had taught us the wrong reply.

"Oh, poor Thowin!" she gasped, as she put both hands over her ears.

Just then I heard Thowin's tremulous answer, "No."

With an angry exclamation, the woman gave her a hard spanking. Then she stopped to say something. Judéwin said it was this: "Are you going to obey my word the next time?"

Thowin answered again with the only word at her command, "No."

This time the woman meant her blows to smart, for the poor frightened girl shrieked at the top of her voice. In the midst of the whipping the blows ceased abruptly, and the woman asked another question: "Are you going to fall in the snow again?"

Thowin gave her bad passwood another trial. We heard her say feebly,

"No! No!"

With this the woman hid away her half-worn slipper, and led the child out, stroking her black shorn head. Perhaps it occurred to her that brute force is not the solution for such a problem. She did nothing to Judéwin nor to me. She only returned to us our unhappy comrade, and left us alone in the room.

During the first two or three seasons misunderstandings as ridiculous as this one of the snow episode frequently took place, bringing unjustifiable frights and punishments into our little lives.

Within a year I was able to express myself somewhat in broken English. As soon as I comprehended a part of what was said and done, a mischievous spirit of revenge possessed me. One day I was called in from my play for some misconduct. I had disregarded a rule which seemed to me very needlessly binding. I was sent into the kitchen to mash the turnips for dinner. It was noon, and steaming dishes were hastily carried into the dining-room. I hated turnips, and their odor which came from the brown jar was offensive to me. With fire in my heart, I took the wooden tool that the paleface woman held out to me. I stood upon a step, and, grasping the handle with both hands, I bent in hot rage over the turnips. I worked my vengeance upon them. All were so busily occupied that no one noticed me. I saw that the turnips were in a pulp, and that further beating could not improve them; but the order was, "Mash these turnips," and mash them I would! I renewed my energy; and as I sent the masher into the bottom of the jar, I felt a satisfying sensation that the weight of my body had gone into it.

Just here a paleface woman came up to my table. As she looked into the jar, she shoved my hands roughly aside. I stood fearless and angry. She placed her red hands upon the rim of the jar. Then she gave one lift and stride away from the table. But lo! the pulpy contents fell through the crumbled bottom to the floor

I She spared me no scolding phrases that I had earned. I did not heed them. I felt triumphant in my revenge, though deep within me I was a wee bit sorry to have broken the jar.

As I sat eating my dinner, and saw that no turnips were served, I whooped in my heart for having once asserted the rebellion within me.

IV.
THE DEVIL.

Among the legends the old warriors used to tell me were many stories of evil spirits. But I was taught to fear them no more than those who stalked about in material guise. I never knew there was an insolent chieftain among the bad spirits, who dared to array his forces against the Great Spirit, until I heard this white man's legend from a paleface woman.

Out of a large book she showed me a picture of the white man's devil. I looked in horror upon the strong claws that grew out of his fur-covered fingers. His feet were like his hands. Trailing at his heels was a scaly tail tipped with a serpent's open jaws. His face was a patchwork: he had bearded cheeks, like some I had seen palefaces wear; his nose was an eagle's bill, and his sharp-pointed ears were pricked up like those of a sly fox. Above them a pair of cow's horns curved upward. I trembled with awe, and my heart throbbed in my throat, as I looked at the king of evil spirits. Then I heard the paleface woman say that this terrible creature roamed loose in the world, and that little girls who disobeyed school regulations were to be tortured by him.

That night I dreamt about this evil divinity. Once again I seemed to be in my mother's cottage. An Indian woman had come to visit my mother. On opposite sides of the kitchen stove, which stood in the center of the small house, my mother and her guest were seated in straight-backed chairs. I played with a train of empty spools hitched together on a string. It was night, and the wick burned feebly. Suddenly I heard some one turn our door-knob from without.

My mother and the woman hushed their talk, and both

94

looked toward the door. It opened gradually. I waited behind the stove. The hinges squeaked as the door was slowly, very slowly pushed inward.

Then in rushed the devil! He was tall! He looked exactly like the picture I had seen of him in the white man's papers. He did not speak to my mother, because he did not know the Indian language, but his glittering yellow eyes were fastened upon me. He took long strides around the stove, passing behind the woman's chair. I threw down my spools, and ran to my mother. He did not fear her, but followed closely after me. Then I ran round and round the stove, crying aloud for help. But my mother and the woman seemed not to know my danger. They sat still, looking quietly upon the devil's chase after me. At last I grew dizzy. My head revolved as on a hidden pivot. My knees became numb, and doubled under my weight like a pair of knife blades without a spring. Beside my mother's chair I fell in a heap. Just as the devil stooped over me with outstretched claws my mother awoke from her quiet indifference, and lifted me on her lap. Whereupon the devil vanished, and I was awake.

On the following morning I took my revenge upon the devil. Stealing into the room where a wall of shelves was filled with books, I drew forth The Stories of the Bible. With a broken slate pencil I carried in my apron pocket, I began by scratching out his wicked eyes. A few moments later, when I was ready to leave the room, there was a ragged hole in the page where the picture of the devil had once been.

V.
IRON ROUTINE

A loud-clamoring bell awakened us at half-past six in the cold winter mornings. From happy dreams of Western rolling lands and unlassoed freedom we tumbled out upon chilly bare floors back again into a paleface day. We had short time to jump into our shoes and clothes, and wet our eyes with icy water, before a small hand bell was vigorously rung for roll call.

There were too many drowsy children and too numerous

orders for the day to waste a moment in any apology to nature for giving her children such a shock in the early morning. We rushed downstairs, bounding over two high steps at a time, to land in the assembly room.

A paleface woman, with a yellow-covered roll book open on her arm and a gnawed pencil in her hand, appeared at the door. Her small, tired face was coldly lighted with a pair of large gray eyes.

She stood still in a halo of authority, while over the rim of her spectacles her eyes pried nervously about the room. Having glanced at her long list of names and called out the first one, she tossed up her chin and peered through the crystals of her spectacles to make sure of the answer "Here."

Relentlessly her pencil black-marked our daily records if we were not present to respond to our names, and no chum of ours had done it successfully for us. No matter if a dull headache or the painful cough of slow consumption had delayed the absentee, there was only time enough to mark the tardiness. It was next to impossible to leave the iron routine after the civilizing machine had once begun its day's buzzing; and as it was inbred in me to suffer in silence rather than to appeal to the ears of one whose open eyes could not see my pain, I have many times trudged in the day's harness heavy-footed, like a dumb sick brute.

Once I lost a dear classmate. I remember well how she used to mope along at my side, until one morning she could not raise her head from her pillow. At her deathbed I stood weeping, as the paleface woman sat near her moistening the dry lips. Among the folds of the bedclothes I saw the open pages of the white man's Bible. The dying Indian girl talked disconnectedly of Jesus the Christ and the paleface who was cooling her swollen hands and feet.

I grew bitter, and censured the woman for cruel neglect of our physical ills. I despised the pencils that moved automatically, and the one teaspoon which dealt out, from a large bottle, healing to a row of variously ailing Indian children. I blamed the hard-working, well-meaning, ignorant woman who was inculcating in our hearts her superstitious ideas. Though I was sullen in all my little troubles, as soon as I felt better I was ready again to smile upon the cruel woman. Within a week I was again actively testing the chains which tightly bound my individuality like a mummy for burial.

The melancholy of those black days has left so long a shadow that it darkens the path of years that have since gone by. These sad memories rise above those of smoothly grinding school days. Perhaps my Indian nature is the moaning wind which stirs them now for their present record. But, however tempestuous this is within me, it comes out as the low voice of a curiously colored seashell, which is only for those ears that are bent with compassion to hear it.

VI.
FOUR STRANGE SUMMERS.

After my first three years of school, I roamed again in the Western country through four strange summers.

During this time I seemed to hang in the heart of chaos, beyond the touch or voice of human aid. My brother, being almost ten years my senior, did not quite understand my feelings. My mother had never gone inside of a schoolhouse, and so she was not capable of comforting her daughter who could read and write. Even nature seemed to have no place for me. I was neither a wee girl nor a tall one; neither a wild Indian nor a tame one. This deplorable situation was the effect of my brief course in the East, and the unsatisfactory "teenth" in a girl's years.

It was under these trying conditions that, one bright afternoon, as I sat restless and unhappy in my mother's cabin, I caught the sound of the spirited step of my brother's pony on the road which passed by our dwelling. Soon I heard the wheels of a light buckboard, and Dawée's familiar "Ho!" to his pony. He alighted upon the bare ground in front of our house. Tying his pony to one of the projecting corner logs of the low-roofed cottage, he stepped upon the wooden doorstep.

I met him there with a hurried greeting, and, as I passed by, he looked a quiet "What?" into my eyes.

When he began talking with my mother, I slipped the rope from the pony's bridle. Seizing the reins and bracing my feet against the dashboard, I wheeled around in an instant.

The pony was ever ready to try his speed. Looking backward, I saw Dawée waving his hand to me. I turned with the curve in the road and disappeared. I followed the winding road which crawled upward between the bases of little hillocks. Deep water-worn ditches ran parallel on either side. A strong wind blew against my cheeks and fluttered my sleeves. The pony reached the top of the highest hill, and began an even race on the level lands. There was nothing moving within that great circular horizon of the Dakota prairies save the tall grasses, over which the wind blew and rolled off in long, shadowy waves.

Within this vast wigwam of blue and green I rode reckless and insignificant. It satisfied my small consciousness to see the white foam fly from the pony's mouth.

Suddenly, out of the earth a coyote came forth at a swinging trot that was taking the cunning thief toward the hills and the village beyond. Upon the moment's impulse, I gave him a long chase and a wholesome fright. As I turned away to go back to the village, the wolf sank down upon his haunches for rest, for it was a hot summer day; and as I drove slowly homeward, I saw his sharp nose still pointed at me, until I vanished below the margin of the hilltops.

In a little while I came in sight of my mother's house. Dawée stood in the yard, laughing at an old warrior who was pointing his forefinger, and again waving his whole hand, toward the hills. With his blanket drawn over one shoulder, he talked and motioned excitedly. Dawée turned the old man by the shoulder and pointed me out to him.

"Oh, han!" (Oh, yes) the warrior muttered, and went his way. He had climbed the top of his favorite barren hill to survey the surrounding prairies, when he spied my chase after the coyote. His keen eyes recognized the pony and driver. At once uneasy for my safety, he had come running to my mother's cabin to give her warning. I did not appreciate his kindly interest, for there was an unrest gnawing at my heart.

As soon as he went away, I asked Dawée about something else.

"No, my baby sister, I cannot take you with me to the party tonight," he replied. Though I was not far from fifteen, and I felt that before long I should enjoy all the privileges of my tall cousin, Dawée persisted in calling me his baby sister.

That moonlight night, I cried in my mother's presence when I heard the jolly young people pass by our cottage. They were no more young braves in blankets and eagle plumes, nor Indian maids with prettily painted cheeks. They had gone three years to school in the East, and had become civilized. The young men wore the white man's coat and trousers, with bright neckties. The girls wore tight muslin dresses, with ribbons at neck and waist. At these gatherings they talked English. I could speak English almost as well as my brother, but I was not properly dressed to be taken along. I had no hat, no ribbons, and no close-fitting gown. Since my return from school I had thrown away my shoes, and wore again the soft moccasins.

While Dawée was busily preparing to go I controlled my tears. But when I heard him bounding away on his pony, I buried my face in my arms and cried hot tears.

My mother was troubled by my unhappiness. Coming to my side, she offered me the only printed matter we had in our home. It was an Indian Bible, given her some years ago by a missionary. She tried to console me. "Here, my child, are the white man's papers. Read a little from them," she said most piously.

I took it from her hand, for her sake; but my enraged spirit felt more like burning the book, which afforded me no help, and was a perfect delusion to my mother. I did not read it, but laid it unopened on the floor, where I sat on my feet. The dim yellow light of the braided muslin burning in a small vessel of oil flickered and sizzled in the awful silent storm which followed my rejection of the Bible.

Now my wrath against the fates consumed my tears before they reached my eyes. I sat stony, with a bowed head. My mother threw a shawl over her head and shoulders, and stepped out into the night.

After an uncertain solitude, I was suddenly aroused by a loud cry piercing the night. It was my mother's voice wailing among the barren hills which held the bones of buried warriors. She called aloud for her brothers' spirits to support her in her helpless misery. My fingers Grey icy cold, as I realized that my unrestrained tears had betrayed my suffering to her, and she was grieving for me.

Before she returned, though I knew she was on her way, for she had ceased her weeping, I extinguished the light, and leaned my head on the window sill.

Many schemes of running away from my surroundings hovered about in my mind. A few more moons of such a turmoil drove me away to the eastern school. I rode on the white man's iron steed, thinking it would bring me back to my mother in a few winters, when I should be grown tall, and there would be congenial friends awaiting me.

VII.
INCURRING MY MOTHER'S DISPLEASURE.

In the second journey to the East I had not come without some precautions. I had a secret interview with one of our best medicine men, and when I left his wigwam I carried securely in my sleeve a tiny bunch of magic roots. This possession assured me of friends wherever I should go. So absolutely did I believe in its charms that I wore it through all the school routine for more than a year. Then, before I lost my faith in the dead roots, I lost the little buckskin bag containing all my good luck.

At the close of this second term of three years I was the proud owner of my first diploma. The following autumn I ventured upon a college career against my mother's will.

I had written for her approval, but in her reply I found no encouragement. She called my notice to her neighbors' children, who had completed their education in three years. They had returned to their homes, and were then talking English with the frontier settlers. Her few words hinted that I had better give up my slow attempt to learn the white man's ways, and be content to roam over the prairies and find my living upon wild roots. I silenced her by deliberate disobedience.

Thus, homeless and heavy-hearted, I began anew my life among strangers.

As I hid myself in my little room in the college dormitory, away from the scornful and yet curious eyes of the students, I pined for sympathy. Often I wept in secret, wishing I had gone West, to be nourished by my mother's love, instead of remaining among a cold race whose hearts were frozen hard with prejudice.

During the fall and winter seasons I scarcely had a real friend, though by that time several of my classmates were courteous to me at a safe distance.

My mother had not yet forgiven my rudeness to her, and I had no moment for letter-writing. By daylight and lamplight, I spun with reeds and thistles, until my hands were tired from their weaving, the magic design which promised me the white man's respect.

At length, in the spring term, I entered an oratorical contest among the various classes. As the day of competition approached, it did not seem possible that the event was so near at hand, but it came. In the chapel the classes assembled together, with their invited guests. The high platform was carpeted, and gaily festooned with college colors. A bright white light illumined the room, and outlined clearly the great polished beams that arched the domed ceiling. The assembled crowds filled the air with pulsating murmurs. When the hour for speaking arrived all were hushed. But on the wall the old clock which pointed out the trying moment ticked calmly on.

One after another I saw and heard the orators. Still, I could not realize that they longed for the favorable decision of the judges as much as I did. Each contestant received a loud burst of applause, and some were cheered heartily. Too soon my turn came, and I paused a moment behind the curtains for a deep breath. After my concluding words, I heard the same applause that the others had called out.

Upon my retreating steps, I was astounded to receive from my fellow-students a large bouquet of roses tied with flowing ribbons. With the lovely flowers I fled from the stage. This friendly token was a rebuke to me for the hard feelings I had borne them.

Later, the decision of the judges awarded me the first place. Then there was a mad uproar in the hall, where my classmates sang and shouted my name at the top of their lungs; and the disappointed students howled and brayed in fearfully dissonant tin trumpets. In this excitement, happy students rushed forward to offer their congratulations. And I could not conceal a smile when they wished to escort me in a procession to the students' parlor, where all were going to calm themselves. Thanking them for the kind spirit which prompted them to make such a proposition, I walked alone with the night to my own little room.

A few weeks afterward, I appeared as the college representative in another contest. This time the competition was among orators from different colleges in our State. It was held at the State capital, in one of the largest opera houses.

Here again was a strong prejudice against my people. In the evening, as the great audience filled the house, the student bodies began warring among themselves. Fortunately, I was spared witnessing any of the noisy wrangling before the contest began. The slurs against the Indian that stained the lips of our opponents were already burning like a dry fever within my breast.

But after the orations were delivered a deeper burn awaited me. There, before that vast ocean of eyes, some college rowdies threw out a large white flag, with a drawing of a most forlorn Indian girl on it. Under this they had printed in bold black letters words that ridiculed the college which was represented by a "squaw." Such worse than barbarian rudeness embittered me. While we waited for the verdict of the judges, I gleamed fiercely upon the throngs of palefaces. My teeth were hard set, as I saw the white flag still floating insolently in the air.

Then anxiously we watched the man carry toward the stage the envelope containing the final decision.

There were two prizes given, that night, and one of them was mine!

The evil spirit laughed within me when the white flag dropped out of sight, and the hands which hurled it hung limp in defeat.

Leaving the crowd as quickly as possible, I was soon in my room. The rest of the night I sat in an armchair and gazed into the crackling fire. I laughed no more in triumph when thus alone. The little taste of victory did not satisfy a hunger in my heart. In my mind I saw my mother far away on the Western plains, and she was holding a charge against me.

Uncle Sam's Indian Wards

WHAT THE GOVERNMENT IS DOING TO MAKE FIRST-CLASS MEN AND WOMEN OF THE SONS AND DAUGHTERS OF REAL RED MEN—SOME EXCELLENT RESULTS.

By EDWARD B. CLARK

OX WARBLES ATTACK BACKS OF CATTLE

EDITOR'S EXPLANATION FOR
"UNCLE SAM'S INDIAN WARDS"
BY EDWARD B. CLARK

This newspaper article shares a different perspective towards the education of Indigenous children. Clark is in favor of having the children attend different boarding schools to provide them the opportunity to become "civilized" and "educated." He believes that educating the young Indigenous population will solve the "Indian problem" that the United States government is facing and cause them to progress on a path towards civilization (Clark, 1916).

The editors felt it was important to include an image of this newspaper article because it contrasts with Zitkala-Sa's essay, "The School Days of Indian Girl," where she shares her experience attending one of these boarding schools. These conflicting perspectives illustrate that providing an education is not always a generous act, especially when you are forcing children to abandon their culture and community, punishing them when they resist, all in an effort to assimilate them to American culture.

105

WHY I AM A PAGAN

BY ZITKALA-SA

When the spirit swells my breast I love to roam leisurely among the green hills; or sometimes, sitting on the brink of the murmuring Missouri, I marvel at the great blue overhead. With half closed eyes I watch the huge cloud shadows in their noiseless play upon the high bluffs opposite me, while into my ear ripple the sweet, soft cadences of the river's song. Folded hands lie in my lap, for the time forgot. My heart and I lie small upon the earth like a grain of throbbing sand. Drifting clouds and tinkling waters, together with the warmth of a genial summer day, bespeak with eloquence the loving Mystery round about us. During the idle while I sat upon the sunny river brink, I grew somewhat, though my response be not so clearly manifest as in the green grass fringing the edge of the high bluff back of me.

At length retracing the uncertain footpath scaling the precipitous embankment, I seek the level lands where grow the wild prairie flowers. And they, the lovely little folk, soothe my soul with their perfumed breath.

Their quaint round faces of varied hue convince the heart which leaps with glad surprise that they, too, are living symbols of omnipotent thought. With a child's eager eye I drink in the myriad star shapes wrought in luxuriant color upon the green. Beautiful is the spiritual essence they embody.

I leave them nodding in the breeze but take along with me their impress upon my heart. I pause to rest me upon a rock embedded on the side of a foothill facing the low river bottom. Here the Stone-Boy, of whom the American aborigine tells, frolics about, shooting his baby arrows and shouting aloud with glee at the tiny shafts of lightning that flash from the flying arrow-beaks. What an ideal warrior he became, baffling the siege of the pests of all the land till he triumphed over their united attack. And here he lay, -- Invan, our great-great-grandfather, older than the hill he rested on, older than the race of men who love to tell of his wonderful career.

Interwoven with the thread of this Indian legend of the rock, I fain would trace a subtle knowledge of the native folk which enabled them to recognize a kinship to any and all parts of this vast universe. By the leading of an ancient trail, I move toward the Indian village.

With the strong, happy sense that both great and small are so surely enfolded in His magnitude that, without a miss, each has his allotted individual ground of opportunities, I am buoyant with good nature.

Yellow Breast, swaying upon the slender stem of a wild sunflower, warbles a sweet assurance of this as I pass near by. Breaking off the clear crystal song, he turns his wee head from side to side eyeing me wisely as slowly I plod with moccasined feet. Then again he yields himself to his song of joy. Flit, flit hither and yon, he fills the summer sky with his swift, sweet melody. And truly does it seem his vigorous freedom lies more in his little spirit than in his wing.

With these thoughts I reach the log cabin whither I am strongly drawn by the tie of a child to an aged mother. Out bounds my four-footed friend to meet me, frisking about my path with unmistakable delight. Chan is a black shaggy dog, "a thorough bred little mongrel," of whom I am very fond. Chan seems to understand many words in Sioux, and will go to her mat even when I whisper the word, though generally I think she is guided by the tone of the voice. Often she tries to imitate the sliding inflection and long drawn out voice to the amusement of our guests, but her articulation is quite beyond my ear. In both my hands I hold her shaggy head and gaze into her large brown eyes. At once the dilated pupils contract into tiny black dots, as if the roguish spirit within would evade my questioning.

Finally resuming the chair at my desk I feel in keen sympathy with my fellow creatures, for I seem to see clearly again that all are akin.

The racial lines, which once were bitterly real, now

serve nothing more than marking out a living mosaic of human beings. And even here men of the same color are like the ivory keys of one instrument where each represents all the rest, yet varies from them in pitch and quality of voice. And those creatures who are for a time mere echoes of another's note are not unlike the fable of the thin sick man whose distorted shadow, dressed like a real creature, came to the old master to make him follow as a shadow. Thus with a compassion for all echoes in human guise, I greet the solemn-faced "native preacher" whom I find awaiting me. I listen with respect for God's creature, though he mouth most strangely the jangling phrases of a bigoted creed.

As our tribe is one large family, where every person is related to all the others, he addressed me: --

"Cousin, I came from the morning church service to talk with you."

"Yes," I said interrogatively, as he paused for some word from me.

Shifting uneasily about in the straight-backed chair he sat upon, he began: "Every holy day (Sunday) I look about our little God's house, and not seeing you there, I am disappointed. This is why I come to-day. Cousin, as I watch you from afar, I see no unbecoming behavior and hear only good reports of you, which all the more burns me with the wish that you were a church member. Cousin, I was taught long years ago by kind missionaries to read the holy book. These godly men taught me also the folly of our old beliefs.

"There is one God who gives reward or punishment to the race of dead men. In the upper region the Christian dead are gathered in unceasing song and prayer. In the deep pit below, the sinful ones dance in torturing flames.

"Think upon these things, my cousin, and choose now to avoid the after-doom of hell fire!" Then followed a long silence in which he clasped tighter and unclasped again his interlocked fingers.

Like instantaneous lightning flashes came pictures of my own mother's making, for she, too, is now a follower of the new superstition.

"Knocking out the chinking of our log cabin, some evil hand thrust in a burning taper of braided dry grass, but failed of his intent, for the fire died out and the half burned brand fell inward to the floor. Directly above it, on a shelf, lay the holy book. This is what we found after our return from a several days' visit. Surely some great power is hid in the sacred book!"

Brushing away from my eyes many like pictures, I offered midday meal to the converted Indian sitting wordless and with downcast face. No sooner had he risen from the table with "Cousin, I have relished it," than the church bell rang.

Thither he hurried forth with his afternoon sermon. I watched him as he hastened along, his eyes bent fast upon the dusty road till he disappeared at the end of a quarter of a mile.

The little incident recalled to mind the copy of a missionary paper brought to my notice a few days ago, in which a "Christian" pugilist commented upon a recent article of mine, grossly perverting the spirit of my pen. Still I would not forget that the pale-faced missionary and the hoodooed aborigine are both God's creatures, though small indeed their own conceptions of Infinite Love. A wee child toddling in a wonder world, I prefer to their dogma my excursions into the natural gardens where the voice of the Great Spirit is heard in the twittering of birds, the rippling of mighty waters, and the sweet breathing of flowers. If this is Paganism, then at present, at least, I am a Pagan.

Invocation

By Jane Johnston Schoolcraft

Rise bravest chief! of the mark of the noble deer,
    With eagle glance,
    Resume thy lance,
And wield again thy warlike spear!
    The foes of thy line,
    With coward design,
Have dared with black envy to garble the truth,
And stain with a falsehood thy valorous youth.
They say when a child, thou wert ta'en from the Sioux,
    And with impotent aim,
    To lessen thy fame
Thy warlike lineage basely abuse;
    For they know that our band,
    Tread a far distant land,
And thou noble chieftain art nerveless and dead,
Thy bow all unstrung, and thy proud spirit fled.
Can the sports of thy youth, or thy deeds ever fade?
    Or those e'er forget,
    Who are mortal men yet,
The scenes where so bravely thou'st lifted the blade,
    Who have fought by thy side,
    And remember thy pride,
When rushing to battle, with valour and ire,
Thou saw'st the fell foes of thy nation expire?
Can the warrior forget how sublimely you rose?
    Like a star in the west,
    When the sun's sink to rest,
That shines in bright splendour to dazzle our foes?
    Thy arm and thy yell,
    Once the tale could repel
Which slander invented, and minions detail,
And still shall thy actions refute the false tale.
Rest thou, noblest chief! in thy dark house of clay,

Thy deeds and thy name,
Thy child's child shall proclaim,
And make the dark forests resound with the lay;
Though thy spirit has fled,
To the hills of the dead,
Yet thy name shall be held in my heart's warmest core,
And cherish'd till valour and love be no more.

Santee Sioux women possibly photographed by C.L. Hamilton

Authors Biographies

Edward S. Curtis was born in 1868 and died in 1952. He served as a photographer's apprentice at the age of 17, where he honed his craft. Two years into his apprenticeship, his family moved to Seattle, Washington, where he bought his own camera and began his career taking photos of the American West, with a significant focus on Native American people. During his career, he took thousands of photographs of Native Americans, and had his own photography studio in Los Angeles, California.

The company Underwood & Underwood was created in 1881 by brothers Elmer Underwood (1859-1947) and Bert Elias Underwood (1862-1943) in Ottawa, Kansas, before moving the company to New York City in 1891. Underwood & Underwood was an early producer and distributor of stereoscopic and other photographic images. At one point, the company was the largest publisher of stereo views in the world, with 10 million views a year.

Kutcahanauu was born in approximately 1873 and his death date is unknown. He was a Native American artist, also known by the name White Bear, who drew pictures of the Hopi Katcinas people. Kutcahanauu was hired by American anthropologist Jesse Walter Fewkes to depict hundreds of individuals from his tribe, the Katcinas. His illustrations are symbolic drawings of individuals, living things, spirits, natural phenomena, and concepts, and their creation is dated back to 1903.

Truman Michelson was born in 1879 in New Rochelle, New York and died in 1938 in Washington D.C. He was a linguist and anthropologist who conducted extensive field research on North American Indigenous languages. Much of his research was focused on languages of the Algonquian family, and the language and culture of the Fox tribe.

Harry Lincoln was a member of the Meskwaki tribe, and assisted anthropologist Truman Michelson with his studies on the Meskwaki culture. He helped Truman with the transcription of the text "How Meskwaki Children Should Be Brought Up", which is included in this anthology. The Meskwaki are an Indigenous group, also known as the Fox tribe. They lived in the Great Lakes region before Euro-American colonization and settlement forced them to move to the Midwest.

Zitkala-Sa was born on the Yankton Indian Reservation in South Dakota in 1876 and died in 1938. She was a writer, activist, musician, and translator. During her childhood, white missionaries came to the Yankton Indian Reservation and she was sent to a missionary school. The effects of this forced assimilation are noted in *The School Days of an Indian Girl.* Zitkala-Sa began her activism work at the mission school and gave a notable speech on women's rights at her graduation. She then worked at Carlisle Indian Industrial School and wrote many articles criticizing missionary schools, which resulted in her dismissal, after which her most famous works *Old Indian Legends* and "Why I Am A Pagan" were written.

Photographer **Charles Lewis Hamilton** was born in approximately 1837 in Kentucky. His brothers, Grant and James H. Hamilton were also photographers. The family fled Missouri during the Civil War and Charles Lewis Hamiltion settled in Fort Randall, South Dakota. Most of his photographs were taken of the Yankton and Santee Tribes located nearby. It is believed that he later moved to Nebraska and died in the Black Hills.

Emily Pauline Johnson (Tekahionwake) was born in 1863 and died in 1917. She and her father were part of the Mohawk tribe. After her father died, she ended up using her writings and performances to support her family. Being of mixed blood gave her writing a unique perspective of having both insider and outsider ideas that concerned Native Americans.

Eli L. Huggins was a United States Army officer born in 1842 and died in 1929. His parents were assistant missionaries for Native American communities in Nicollet County, Minnesota when he was a child. Huggins led a life full of military service and war, which began when he enlisted in the Army at the age of 18. He became fluent in many languages, including the Sioux, and published 31 works in his lifetime. He received the Medal of Honor for catching the Ogallala Sioux Indians by surprise during the Indian Wars in 1888. Some of the Native American men he battled against were Rain-in-the-Face, Iron Shield, and Spotted Eagle.

William Edgar Brown (Nwah-Ke-Nah-Go-Zid) was a member of the Ojibwe tribe. Brown wrote [italicize] Indian Legendary Poems and Songs of Cheer, in addition to [italicize] Echoes of the Forest: American Indian Legends, which contains several texts that are featured within this anthology. The Ojibwe lived mainly in southern Canada and the northern Midwestern portion of the United States. They spoke a form of the Algonquian language and were primarily hunters and fishermen.

Margaret Compton was born in 1852 and died in 1903. She compiled research from the Smithsonian Institute and United States government reports in order to create accurate depictions of Native American fairy tales, which are among five other publications that she authored. Their topics cover Native American stories, cooking, genealogy, and civics.

Charles A. Eastman was born in 1858 with the name Hakadah, and died in 1939. At the time of one of his first life passages, he was renamed Ohiye S'a, before later claiming Charles Eastman as his Christian name. He attended Boston University's medical school, where he became one of the first Native Americans certified as a European-style doctor. In addition to being a lecturer and writer, he advocated for Native rights, practiced medicine for people on reservations in South Dakota, and founded 32 Native American chapters of the YMCA and Boy Scouts. Eastman published some of his writing in order to financially support his family, and he is considered to be the first Native American to publish pieces on American history.

James Athearn Jones was born in Massachusetts in 1791 and died in 1854. He practiced law in New York City in 1822 and was involved in various journals and newspapers, including the United States Library Gazette. Jones himself wasn't Indigenous, but he traveled among the Native American tribes, recording their folklore and tales. He was known to have said that he wanted his work to be as authentic as possible and he would be considered an ethnologist in modern times.

Henry W. Longfellow was born in 1807 and died in 1882. He is one of the most famous poets of his time; some of his most noted works are *Evangeline*, "Paul Revere's Ride," and "I Heard The Bells On Christmas Day." Included in this anthology, *The Song of Hiawatha* was more unusual for the time, as it tells the story of an Ojibwe warrior, Hiawatha, and his love, Minnehaha. This story was partially inspired by Longfellow's friendship with Ojibwe leader George Copway (Kah-Ge-Ga-Gah-Bowh) and Sauk leader Black Hawk (Ma-ka-tai-me-she-kia-kiak). Longfellow's daily life influenced his works, which can be seen in *Poems of Slavery*, written from his abolitionist point of view.

Paul Greer was born in 1887 and died in 1980. The papers of Paul Greer are a collection of his work as a newspaper editor, as well as other personal writing, which focused on agriculture, conservation, senior citizens, and other relevant topics of the time. He worked as an editor for the Omaha Bee, a publication which published writing about Native Americans in Nebraska.

Ely S. Parker was born in 1828 within the Seneca tribe on the Tonawanda Indian Reservation, and he died in 1895. Wishing to succeed in the white world, he adopted the name Ely S. Parker, from his native name Donehogawa. As a teenager, he was chosen to meet with the president of the United States to discuss selling reservation lands to private landowners. Parker studied law in New York, but because he was not recognized as a citizen, he was not allowed to take the bar exam, so he became an engineer and served with General Ulysses S. Grant on his staff as the first Native American Commissioner of Indian Affairs. Parker also made a living on Wall Street and served as an engineer for the New York City Police Department.

Edward B. Clark was born around 1898 and died in 1918 of influenza. He was a journalist for the North Platte Semi-Weekly Tribune, a Nebraska newspaper published in North Platte, Nebraska from 1895-1922. The newspaper was described as having Republican politics and published stories about all major happenings in the area, including several Indian raids and wars, most notably, the Plum Creek Massacre at Fort McPherson.

Jane Johnston Schoolcraft was born in 1800 and died in 1842. She was a member of the Ojibwe Tribe and is considered one of the first Native American authors. She studied literature under her father, and they shared a passion for poetry and history. In 1823, she married Henry Rowe Schoolcraft, and they published a literary magazine together.

Additional Information & Resources

Indigenous communities have been profoundly affected by the arrival of Europeans and unfortunately, are continuing to be affected by colonization. This final section of the anthology contains some information about several prominent issues that are currently affecting Indigenous communities in North America, along with the contact information for different organizations and funds that are working to help them.

Missing and Murdered Indigenous Women (MMIW)

One of the current issues that Indigenous communities are facing is the epidemic of missing and murdered women within their communities. Indigenous women are much more likely to experience violence than any other demographic, with the murder rates being 10 times higher than the national average. It is unlikely that we will ever know the true number of women that have been affected by this issue because of limited resources and the poor data collection done by numerous cities (MMIWG2S, 2020).

There are several organizations such as the Coalition to Stop Violence Against Native Women that are working hard to combat this issue. Their goal is to help prevent violence against Native women by working for social change in their communities by providing support, education, and advocacy to create violence-free communities. For more information about this organization, or for ways to donate, check out their website at www.csvanw.org

Covid-19 Pandemic

The coronavirus has been strongly affecting Indigenous communities. A report conducted by the Centers for Disease Control and Prevention found that Native Americans are among the racial and ethnic minority groups at a higher risk for severe

121

Covid-19 outcomes. This is due to racial inequity and historical trauma that have created disparities in health, and socioeconomic factors between Indigenous and white populations that have had a negative impact on their communities (CDC, 2020).

There are several organizations such as the Covid-19: Emergency Response Fund who provide care and relief to these communities. This fund was developed to provide resources to Native nonprofit organizations and programs that have been heavily impacted by the coronavirus. Some of these high-concentration areas are California, New Mexico, the Pacific Northwest, New York, Navajo Nation, Hopi Tribe, and other Covid-19 hotspots. For more information about this fund, or for ways to donate, check out their website at www.firstnations.org/covid-19-emergency-response-fund.

Additional Resources

Native American Aid is an organization that sponsors programs to help combat poverty on reservations along with addressing different needs among children, adults, and elderly Native Americans on the Northern Plains. To learn more information about ways to volunteer or how to donate visit their website at www.nativepartnership.org/

Legal Aid of Nebraska has a section on their website of links to resources and aid for Indigenous communities. For more information about the resources available, visit their website at www.legalaidofnebraska.org/how-we-help/resources/native-american/.

The Nebraska Indian Child Welfare Coalition (NICWC) is an organization created by the Omaha, Ponca, Santee Sioux, and Winnebago Tribes of Nebraska along with other legal and social service advocates to uphold the Indian Child Welfare Act (ICWA). Their mission is to advocate and raise awareness to help protect Native children's rights and cultural connections. For more information about this organization, visit NICWC.org

Works Cited

CDC. "CDC Data Show Disproportionate Covid-19 Impact in American Indian/Alaska Native Populations." Centers for Disease Control and Prevention, 19 Aug. 2020, www.cdc.gov/media/releases/2020/p0819-covid-19-impact-american-indian-alaska-native.html.

First Nations. "COVID-19 Emergency Response Fund." First Nations Development Institute, 21 Sept. 2020, www.firstnations.org/covid-19-emergency-response-fund/.

Coalition to STOP Violence Against Women. "MMI-WG2S." CSVANW Coalition to STOP Violence Against Women, www.csvanw.org/mmiw/. Accessed 14 Oct. 2020.

Legal Aid of Nebraska. "Native American." Legal Aid of Nebraska, 19 Mar. 2019, www.legalaidofnebraska.org/how-we-help/resources/native-american/.

Native American Aid. NAA Home-Native American Aid, 2015. www.nativepartnership.org/site/PageServer?pagename=naa_index.

Nebraska Indian Child Welfare Coalition Inc. NICWC, nicwc.org/. Accessed 16 Oct. 2020.

Appendix of Sources

Big Winnebago Jim. 1868-1880. Library of Congress, doi: cph.3c15033. Stereograph.

Bonnin, Gertrude (Zitkala-Sa). "*The Badger and the Bear.*" Old Indian Legends, Ginn & Company, 1901. Project Gutenberg, www.gutenberg.org/files/338/338-h/338-h.htm. Accessed 8 Oct. 2020.

Bonnin, Gertrude (Zitkala-Sa). "The School Days of an Indian *Girl.*" *American Indian Stories*, Hayworth Publishing House, 1921. Project Gutenberg, www.gutenberg.org/cache/epub/10376/pg10376-images.html. Accessed 5 Oct. 2020.

Bonnin, Gertrude (Zitkala-Sa). "Why I Am a Pagan." *Atlantic Monthly 90, 1902, pp. 801-803.* Electronic Text Center, University of Virginia Library, www.web.archive.org/web/2 0110212153707/http:/etext.lib.virginia.edu/etcbin/toccer-new2?id=ZitPaga.sgm&images=images/modeng&data=/texts/english/modeng/parsed&tag=public&part=1&division=div1. Accessed 9 Oct. 2020.

Brown, William Edgar. "*Algonquin Love Song.*" Echoes of the forest, American Indian Legends, *The Gorham Press, 1918, pp. 30-31.* The Library of Congress, doi: 1043025050. Accessed 4 Oct. 2020.

Brown, William Edgar. "Legend of the North Star: An Ojibwe Legend." *Echoes of the forest, American Indian Legends,* The Gorham Press, 1918, pp. 163-167. *The Library of Congress,* doi: 1043025050. Accessed 5 Oct. 2020.

Brown, William Edgar. "Why The Pine Trees Weep: An Ojibwe Legend." *Echoes of the forest, American Indian Legends,* The

Gorham Press, 1918, pp. 181-185.] *The Library of Congress,* doi: 1043025050. Accessed 4 Oct. 2020.

Clark, Edward B. "Uncle Sam's Indian Wards." *The North Platte semi-weekly tribune.* (North Platte, Neb.), 25 Feb. 1916.*Chronicling America: Historic American Newspapers.* Library of Congress, www.chroniclingamerica.loc.gov/lccn.2010270504/1916-02-25/ed-1/seq-6/.

Compton, Margaret. "The Star Maiden." *American Indian Fairy Tales,* Dodd, *Mead, & Company, 1907.* Sacred Texts, www.sacred-texts.com/nam/ait/ait12.htm. Accessed 9 Oct. 2020.

Curtis, Edward S. "*Kotsuis and Hohhug--Nakoaktok, wearing ceremonial dress, with long beaks, on their haunches, dancing (?)].*" 1914. Library of Congress, doi: cph.3c08464. 1 photographic print.

Eastman, Charles A. (Ohiyesa). "First Impressions of Civilization." [italicize] Indian Boyhood, [normal text] McClure, Phillips & Co., 1902. [italicize] Project Gutenberg, [normal text] http://www.gutenberg.org/files/337/337-h/337-h.htm. Accessed 9 Oct. 2020.

Eastman, Charles A. (Ohiyesa). "My Indian Grandmother." Indian Boyhood, *McClure, Phillips & Co., 1902.* Project Gutenberg, http://www.gutenberg.org/files/337/337-h/337-h.htm. Accessed 9 Oct. 2020.

Greer, Paul. "Lo The Poor Indian Prospers." Omaha daily bee (Omaha, Neb.), 26 Sept. 1920. *Nebraska Newspapers. University of Nebraska-Lincoln Libraries,* www.nebnewspapers.unl.ed u/lccn/sn99021999/1920-09-26/ed-1/seq-29 /#words=Indian+Indians. Accessed 9 Oct. 2020.

Hamilton, C. L. (?). Santee Sioux women. 1868-1880. Library of Congress, doi: cph.3c15042. Stereograph. Accessed 9 Oct. 2020.
Hamilton, C. L. (?). Three Winnebago women, one with child on her back, on hillside. 1868-1880. Library of Congress, doi: cph.3c15045. Stereograph. Accessed 9 Oct. 2020.

Hamilton, C.L. (?). Winnebago camp scene. 1868-1880. Library of Congress, doi: cph.3c15046. Stereograph. Accessed 9 Oct. 2020.

Johnson, E. Pauline. "As Red Men Die." The White Wampum, Lamson, Wolffe & Co., 1895. Project Gutenberg, www.gutenberg.org/files/52988/52988-h/52988-h.htm. Accessed 9 Oct. 2020.

Johnson, E. Pauline. "Through Time and Bitter Distance." 1912. Poets.org, www.poets.org/poem/through-time-and-bitter-distance. Accessed 8 Oct. 2020.

Jones, James Athearn. "The Mother of the World: A Tradition of the Dog-Ribs." Traditions of the North American Indians, Vol. 1, *Colburn and Bentley, 1820.* Project Gutenberg, www.gutenberg.org/files/20826/20826-h/20826-h.htm. Accessed 8 Oct. 2020

Kutcahanauu (White-Bear). "Hopi katcinas drawn by native artists." *1903.* Hopi katcinas drawn by native artists, edited by Jesse Walter Fewkes, Washington, 1903, p. 142. Library of Congress, doi: cph.3c08464. Illustrations. Accessed 8 Oct. 2020.

Kutcahanauu (White-Bear). "Hopi katcinas drawn by native artists." *1903.* Hopi katcinas drawn by native artists, edited by Jesse Walter Fewkes, Washington, 1903, p. 147. Library of Congress, doi: cph.3c08464. Illustrations. Accessed 8 Oct. 2020.

Longfellow, Henry W. "Hiawatha's Wooing." The Song of Hiawatha, Ticknor and Fields, 1855. Project Gutenberg, www.gutenberg.org/files/19/19-h/19-h.htm#Xchap. Accessed 5 Oct. 2020.

Michelson, Truman. "How Meskwaki Children Should Be Brought Up." American Indian life, B.W. Huebsch Inc., 1922. Project Gutenberg, www.gutenberg.org/files/59968/59968-h/59968-h.htm#MESKAWI_CHILDREN. Accessed 9 Oct. 2020.

Parker, Ely S. "Document: Letter to Harriet Converse." 1885. Teaching American History, www.teachingamericanhistory.org/library/document/letter-to-harriet-converse/. Accessed 8 Oct. 2020.

Schoolcraft, Jane Johnston. "Invocation." The Literary Voyager, 1827. Poets.org, www.poets.org/poem/invocation. Accessed 8 Oct. 2020.

Underwood & Underwood. "The Masked Kachinas (Hopi Indian "Rain-makers"). 1903. Library of Congress, doi: cph.3b05011. Stereograph.

About the Members of Happy Cloud Press

Jonelle Alvarado (**Managing Editor**) Jonelle is a senior from Omaha, Nebraska who is majoring in English and Communication Studies. After graduation, Jonelle hopes to enter the publishing industry. She is a proud member of the Delta Xi Nu Multicultural Sorority Inc. at the University of Nebraska-Lincoln. In her free time, she enjoys watching Netflix and reading various novels.

Cecelia Bialas (**Copy Editor**) Cecelia is an English major from Milford, Nebraska. After graduating, she plans on working in the trade publishing industry, acquiring and reviewing manuscripts. Her favorite things to read are poetry, historical fiction, and women's fiction. She is a member of the UNL Equestrian Team, an editor for Laurus, and spends her free time riding horses, raising awareness for chronic illness on Instagram, reading, hiking, and kayaking.

Tessa Faust (**Design Director**) Tessa is majoring in Classics and Religious Studies. With class and university clubs like Spectrum and Classics Club, she keeps quite busy. In her free time, she likes to play board games with friends, or watch horror movies and anime. After graduation, Tessa hopes to continue her education or find a job in the non-profit sector.

Sarah Kee (**Acquisitions Editor**) Sarah is a junior from Omaha, Nebraska who is an English major with minors in Spanish and Mathematics. She is an editor for Laurus, and a member of the University of Nebraska-Lincoln Honors Program and Creative Commons. After graduation, Sarah plans on pursuing a career in the publishing industry. When Sarah isn't in class, she's either studying, tutoring other students, or watching Netflix shows with her roommates.

Stone McGuire (Marketing Director) Stone is a senior English major with minors in History and Political Science. Stone grew up in the northwestern part of Montana. After graduation, as a first-generation student, Stone plans to pursue a career in writing. He is a member of the University of Nebraska-Lincoln Student Veterans Organization, and spends his free time playing guitar, exercising, reading, writing, and camping.